A NEW CUT IN GENES

Howe peered into Kent's eyes. "This jar contains none other than the Fluid of Life, Baron. This elixir requires only one remaining ingredient in order to be complete. One, Baron, and I'll be disappointed in you, sir, if you cannot predict what that is."

Kent sighed, "Me."

Howe laughed evilly, applauded soundlessly. "Almost, almost. You, of course, but not all of you."

"Why not take all of me?"

"All I need is one of your organs. A little puree into the Fluid of Life, a little blending of the gene pool in the deep end, and . . ."

Kent got it and wished he hadn't, and said, "And you're going to create a mate for the horny bastard outside."

Howe applauded. "Wonderful, Mr. Montana, wonderful."

"CRAIG-SHAW-GARDNERESQUE . . . Fans of the Ebenezum and Cineverse books will, in fact, certainly enjoy this one."
—Raymond's Reviews

Ace Books by Lionel Fenn

KENT MONTANA AND THE REALLY UGLY THING FROM MARS
KENT MONTANA AND THE REASONABLY INVISIBLE MAN
KENT MONTANA AND THE ONCE AND FUTURE THING

KENT MONTANA AND THE ONCE AND FUTURE THING

LIONEL FENN

ACE BOOKS, NEW YORK

This book is an Ace original edition,
and has never been previously published.

KENT MONTANA AND THE
ONCE AND FUTURE THING

An Ace book / published by arrangement with
the author

PRINTING HISTORY
Ace edition / August 1991

ISBN: 0-441-43537-8

Ace Books are published by The Berkley Publishing Group,
200 Madison Avenue, New York, New York 10016.
The name "ACE" and the "A" logo
are trademarks belonging to Charter Communications, Inc.

PRINTED IN THE UNITED STATES OF AMERICA

10 9 8 7 6 5 4 3 2 1

As everyone knows, the primordial swamp contains many secrets which, over the course of time, have been the target of many a courageous, albeit foolhardy, adventurer seeking to uncover the Truth;

As everyone knows, the primordial swamp does not easily, if ever, surrender those secrets to those adventurers who trespass upon its watery domain;

As everyone knows, stuff happens in those primordial swamps you wouldn't wish on your worst enemy unless he's been really rotten, in which case even the primordial swamp can't hold a candle to a good poke in the eye with a sharp stick.

All of which proves that if I had written this book, it would have had a lot more sex in it.

> —Simon Lake
> (twin brother of Timothy Boggs and younger brother of Lionel Fenn and Geoffrey Marsh. Mr. Lake is the real author of the YA novel *Fire Mask*, though it was published under the pseudonym Charles Grant because they thought his real name was too fishy.)

– I –

Howe's Landing

◆ 1 ◆

The depot wasn't much as depots go, being little more than a fairly large, nearly square, sun-bleached wood-and-stone building with a couple of iron-frame benches inside and out, a ticket office with a barred window that hardly anybody ever sat behind, and a drooping shingle roof over a platform that served the infrequent trains in both directions. But the townspeople were willing to put up with it as long as it didn't catch fire, breed rats, or bring temporary sanctuary to unsavory types who might bring disgrace and blasphemy upon the community.

It was Silas Bouquette's job to make sure that tradition endured well unto the fourth or fifth generation.

He was a tall man, lean to the point of ridiculous, cleanshaven, bulbous-eyed, wispy-haired and never without the well-oiled and always loaded revolver his granddaddy had given him on his deathbed.

"Keep watch," the old man had wheezed wetly from his mattress while bottle flies hovered noisily in the window. "You keep watch, boy, y'hear?"

"Yes sir, Granddaddy," Silas had answered solemnly.

"You keep an eye on ever person what comes off that there train." A scrawny but powerful hand gripped the young man's arm. "You watch!"

"I will, I will!" Silas had vowed.

The old man sagged back onto his straw pillow. "It's comin', boy, it's comin'. I know it. I seen the signs. I heared the calls out there in the bayou." He coughed. Under the house an alligator coughed in sympathy. A mangy coon dog howled in sorrow in the overgrown yard. "I . . ."

Silas waited.

The old man sighed.

Without a twinge of conscience, Silas hoped the old man was dead. He had been on the death watch for three weeks now, and the old buzzard hadn't let go yet. It was getting embarrassing.

The sunken chest shuddered. Rose. Subsided. Rose again so slowly it barely disturbed the air.

Pale, dry lips trembled.

Silas leaned closer. "Granddaddy? Granddaddy, you all right?"

"I'm dying," was the hoarse, faint reply.

"Well, I know that, Granddaddy, but are you all right?"

Eyelids like dried paper fluttered. Eyes like milky blue marbles stared at the bare ceiling. "Silas?"

"Here, Granddaddy."

"You keep watch."

Silas nodded a solemn vow even though he knew the old coot couldn't see him; he also hefted the ancient but eminently serviceable revolver, spun it around, aimed, and blushed with shame for thinking what he was thinking when he ought to have been thinking about something else, like the old geezer having the sense to die before the next crop came in.

The eyes closed; the lips calmed; the alligator crawled from under the house and ate the coon dog.

Silas waited.

The old man whimpered as if caught in a bad dream.

The wind soughed.

Silas shifted uneasily in the three-legged wooden chair he'd brought in from the shack's only other room, and stared out the window. Gnarled cypress and gum trees, Spanish moss, high brush that rattled like old bones when the wind blew—it wasn't much of a view, but it was, he thought, better than looking at Samson Bouquette drooling over the hell and gone.

The alligator made its way to the chicken house.

The sun set.

Too many shadows crept into the shack, filled too many spaces where they didn't belong. Silas lit a hurricane lamp and placed it on a rickety table. He was hungry. Hell, he was starving. And by the sound of it, that damn alligator had cleaned out all the chickens.

Then, without warning, the old man sat bolt upright, his eyes wide, his nostrils flaring, his left arm outstretched as he pointed toward his grandson.

"Watch!" Samson cried. "Watch for the—!"

Silas, who had backed hastily into the wall and thunked his skull against it, gaped, gasped, and nearly fled when the old man strangled horribly on his last word, screamed, gurgled, and flopped back onto the mattress.

The funeral had been quiet.

The alligator had fasted.

And Silas, from his position on the platform chair, rocked back against the station house as he wondered who was going to take over this stupid job when he was gone. He had no wife, had no kids, had no kin at all that he was aware of, and nobody seemed interested in becoming a Watcher-in-training, not even Myrtle Mae Beauregard, head of the Landing Militia and Bugle Corps. Fact was, most of Howe's Landing had apparently forgotten why he was there. The schoolchildren made fun of him, the adults tolerated him, and the dogs liked to gnaw on his wooden leg whenever he napped. It was a thankless job, no doubt about it.

But someone had to watch.

Someone had to keep an eye on the trains.

Someone had to make sure that whatever he was watching for didn't creep into town unwatched.

So he shifted, glanced at the clock on the wall in the waiting room, and sighed when he saw that it wouldn't be long before the noon train came in.

A drop of sweat ran down his cheek.

A fat tom wandered across the tracks and vanished into the high weeds on the other side.

Mosquitoes hummed, flies buzzed, a buzzard circled over the trees.

If he had any brains, he'd go home, turn on the air conditioning, the TV, and clip a few coupons.

But he did not leave his post, no matter the temptations. After all, aside from the watching part, and his promise to his granddaddy, he was getting paid pretty damn good. Every week an envelope appeared in his post office box at the General Store and Notion Parlor. Three hundred dollars. Two thirds of which went immediately into his bank account at the First Louisiana Trust over on Main Street, one third of which went into the hand-cranked cash register at Della Depew's by the time he had finished his Friday night drinking with the boys.

He had no idea who sent him the money.

He didn't care.

As soon as he had himself enough money, he was gonna—

"Hey there, Silas."

He opened one eye, peered into the flushed round face of the stationmaster, and closed it again. "Hey, Rude."

"Seen anything today?"

"Nope."

The chubby man flipped out his pocket watch, thumbed open the cover, and squinted. "Be here soon."

"Yep."

"Think today's the day?"

"Don't know."

A hot breeze blew dust across the platform.

"Been waiting a long time, ain't you?"

"Seems like years, to tell the truth."

"Near to ten, maybe fifteen, best I figure."

"Sounds about right."

"Think it's gonna happen?"

Silas inhaled slowly, exhaled a sigh. "Hope not."

The stationmaster agreed with a nod, and squinted northward up the tracks. "No offense, but your granddaddy was nuts, you know."

"Yeah, but he seen it the first time, was there when it ended. The first time." He cocked an eye at his friend. "Can always be a second time."

"Suppose."

"Yep."

A second buzzard joined the first.

Rudy Humpquin blew his nose on a railroad-issue handkerchief and said, "Gonna be a party at the Manor tonight."

Silas nodded. "Heard about it."

"You going?"

They chuckled just shy of slapping their knees. Nobody from the Landing was ever invited to parties up at the Manor. Well, maybe a couple of people. The mayor, idiots like that. But not the likes of Silas and Rudy. They didn't much care. Della Depew's place was good enough for them, and cheaper.

Heavy booted feet climbed the steps at the far end of the platform. Silas leaned around the stationmaster to see who it was, rolled his eyes, and leaned back.

"Hey, Silas. Hey, Rude."

Rudy adjusted his cap. "Hey, Joe Bill."

Silas held his greeting to a curt nod. He hated Joe Bill Spain, couldn't stand the ground the porkass sumbitch walked on. Always strutting around in that dark green polyester uniform with its stupid flathead cap like he owned the damn place, messing with the local girls, making fun of the Landing, when all he ever did was drive that big old gunboat Mercury for Montague Howe, picking up passengers to take out to the Manor, and dropping them off again when they was leaving. He smelled too, always using some kind of foreign-sounding cologne stuff to hide the fact that he was uglier than a possum what lost a duel with a tractor.

Joe Bill leaned against a roof post and peered into the distance. "Train on time, Rude?"

"Find out when she gets here, Joe Bill."

Joe Bill chuckled.

Silas opened one eye and took a quick look, closed it again when he saw that Spain had been lifting again, had more muscles on his muscles that made them polyester seams like to burst if he took a deep breath.

A whistle in the distance.

Joe Bill straightened.

The stationmaster dusted his lapels.

And Silas slowly, quietly, cocked the hammer of his revolver.

The main street of Howe's Landing was several blocks of fairly quiet businesses, a handful of rowdy bars, and a number of homes that, despite the brutal pummeling of the Louisiana sun, always managed to look freshly painted. Cats prowled, dogs napped, children frolicked, people nodded to each other on the sidewalk, old men in pressed white suits sat on shaded benches and played checkers, women gossiped quietly in the beauty parlor, and church bells sounded delightfully languid on humid Sunday mornings.

A prosperous community.

A peaceful community.

Off the beaten track, to be sure; connected with the outside world only by a single well-paved road and the train, of course; and marked on one side by a series of fertile farms and cane fields, on the other three sides by a perfectly functioning ecosystem of swampland which lured tourist and scientist in equal, harmonious measure.

Rural without being cute.

Bucolic without being sleepy.

Rustic without all the straw.

And, thought Myrtle Mae Beauregard, about the most boring goddamn place on the face of this here earth.

So when she heard the train whistle, soft there in the distance, filtering through the magnolia tree on her front lawn like the sound of a lonesome swamp dove crying for its dear departed mate, she immediately stopped her rocking and cocked her head. Against the porch railing a loaded shotgun gleamed in the afternoon sun; against the wall to her right a loaded rifle gleamed in the shade; strapped to the underside of her rocking chair's left armrest a freshly honed bowie knife gleamed.

She frowned as she listened.

She waited as she frowned.

It wasn't that she didn't trust Silas Bouquette to do his job, but she always did like to be prepared.

Although she certainly did not look forward to Hell returning to the land where she had been born and raised, bringing grief, destruction, death, and unwanted media attention, it would definitely be better than spending the rest of her life waiting around for some old codger to leave off his checkers for once and jump her bones.

She sighed, then, for the memory of the good old days, plucked her pipe from between her shriveled lips, and shoved herself out of the chair. A few tottering steps to the railing,

and she leaned forward, glancing up and down the street before
hobbling inside to the wall phone by the front door. She dialed
a number, squinted through the screen door, and said, "Hey,
Gert," when the connection was made.

"Myrtle Mae, that you?"

"Heard the train, Gert."

"Oh Lordy."

"My thigh bone's acting up."

"Oh gracious."

"You ready?"

"Is it today? I got my grandson's birthday today, Myrtle Mae.
Can't be today."

"Never can tell."

"Oh shoo."

"You ready?"

"Well, not exactly."

"What you mean, not exactly?"

"Sam Bob found the Colt under my pillow last week. Took
it away 'fore I could stop him."

"You kick him where I tole you?"

"Tried, but I fell outta my walker."

"Lord's sake, Gert, you can't kick no man in the balls from
a walker, how many times I gotta tell you?"

"Don't matter. He didn't find the Thompson."

"Thank God."

"But I do got the birthday today, Myrtle Mae. This gonna
mess things up."

"Just be near a phone, girl, y'hear? You get my call, you
come running."

Myrtle Mae hung up, cursed fluently in four different bayou
dialects, and dialed again.

"Hey, Ethel June."

"Damn, that you, Myrtle Mae?"

"Train's coming in."

"Look, Myrtle Mae, I got ninety dozen pots steaming at once
here, I can't be fooling around with you."

"Damnit, Ethel June, you hear the code word?"

"Well, no."

"Then don't get yourself all hot, for heaven's sake. I'm just
letting you know the train's coming."

"Well, hell, I can hear that, for god's sake. Damn track runs right by the house, don't it?"

"All I want to know, are you ready?"

"Myrtle Mae, I been ready since World War Two. Now run along, hear? Damn roots are boiling over."

Myrtle Mae scowled at the dial tone, scowled at the wall, scowled when she heard the train's second whistle, signaling that it was about to cross the bridge over Howe's Lake, on the southern end of the bayou. Quickly she hobbled back to the porch, dropped into her rocker, unstrapped the bowie knife, and practiced her moves by slicing bumblebees in half, on the wing, whenever they came too close.

Her left thigh bone ached.

Surely, she thought, this would be the day.

In the sweltering barbershop on the corner of Main and Chaney, Doc Pruit slowly replaced the receiver of the wall phone and dropped into one of the eight wooden chairs along the side wall. His hands trembled until he folded them tightly in his lap; his jaw trembled until he clenched his teeth; the tic that made him wink uncontrollably jumped into action until he clamped his eyes shut.

No one saw him.

Actually, the only other person in the shop was the barber himself, and he was napping solidly in one of the four red-leather chairs, every so often snipping the air with his fingers while he asked his dream-customer how he thought the Saints would do this year.

Emanuel Pruit, on the other hand, had been talking doomsday futures and other profit margin opportunities with his Chicago commodities broker when he'd heard the second whistle, and a sudden chill had stiffened his spine.

He knew that chill.

Lord preserve us, how he knew that chill.

He had had it once before, decades ago, when Howe's Landing had almost become a ghost town thanks to the horrors that had come shambling and clawing their way out of the bayou.

Now it was back.

He knew without bothering to check with Myrtle Mae's thigh bone that the horrors were about to return.

Oh Lord, he thought; oh lord.

The barber muttered something about Edgar Allan Poe and his heathen influence on dirty dancing.

A car backfired outside.

The barber scrambled to his feet and reached for the blow dryer, blushed, nodded to Doc, and dropped back into the chair with a towel over his face.

A sound much like a whimper slipped past Doc's quivering pale lips, where it quickly turned into a venomous curse. He slapped the armrest angrily. He should have known it. By damn, he should have known this would happen sooner or later. He had seen all the signs and had deliberately ignored them, just as he had forty long years ago. Back then he hadn't wanted to believe them, thought in his position as town doctor and part-time veterinarian that they were merely products of highly strung imaginations fueled by superstition, ignorance, and some of that wicked stuff Silas made in his deserted chicken coop. O how he'd learned how wrong he was! And when the signs had reappeared at the end of last winter, and the gossip, and the mustering of Myrtle Mae's crack militia, he had once again turned a blind eye and a deaf ear to what he knew was the truth. But what could he do? He was getting old, he was already washed-up, he was a miserable excuse for a Johns Hopkins graduate, and nobody would listen even if he did decide to sound the alarm.

If anyone had wanted to know the shameful truth, the only reason he had stuck around here lately was Blanche. Blanche Knox. The only woman these days who was able, just by a look and a wink, to bubble his thinning blood. If it hadn't been for her, for her uniform, for her way with patients, for her ingenious ruminations on the erotic possibilities of stirrups and tongue depressors, he would have packed his gear and left for Boise months ago.

Surely she at least had a right to know what he knew; surely she might be spared the approaching bayou Armageddon if he could only locate the hidden lair of his courage and smoke it out into the open without killing the damn thing; surely, by logical and emotional extension, the town had an inalienable right to know about the return of his chill.

The train's third whistle snapped his eyes open.

Ah, the hell with it.

It had nothing to do with him.

These people had used him up, wrung him out, and tossed him away like so much bad seed.

The hell with it.

They didn't deserve to know what he knew.

He reached into his badly wrinkled and ill-fitting suit jacket, pulled out a tarnished silver flask, and unscrewed the top. Without bothering to check if the barber was watching, he drank. And drank again.

The hell with it.

Let the crackers fry.

Young Roger Ace had no intention of tripping Bessy Lou Leigh. It was the farthest thing from his mind. He would have sooner cut his own throat than harm her. But since the day had been pretty rotten right from the beginning, what with his being fired this morning from his chief clerk's job at the five-and-dime and all, he wasn't at all surprised when, in leaving Della Depew's after celebrating the publication of his fifteenth novel, he slipped on a banana peel, fell back against the wall, and in so doing, thrust out his left foot for balance.

Which Bessy Lou promptly tripped over.

Luckily her own balance was more stable, and she managed, after a couple of yards of hopping, spinning, and swearing, to stop, whirl, plant her hands on her generously turned hips, and glare at him.

He smiled sheepishly. "Sorry, Bessy Lou." Hastily, he straightened himself, his tie, his white linen jacket, and his white hat.

She stomped over to him and waggled a delicate finger in his face. "Darn it, Roger, are you drunk again?"

"God no," he protested truthfully. A jerk of his thumb over his shoulder. "A couple of beers, that's all, I swear it." He crossed his heart, kissed his pinky, held it up, and noted the breeze was blowing out of the west this afternoon, not exactly a good sign for those sailing on the swamp. "*Ant Gods of the Antares* came out today." He grinned and yanked a thick paperback book from his inside jacket pocket. "I was celebrating, that's all."

He didn't think he ought to tell her about the getting fired part. Such was not the kind of news a lady wanted to hear about the gentleman who desired more from her than a friendly wave on a Sunday morning, even if she didn't know and he was getting mighty sick of waiting for her to figure it out.

"Celebrating," she repeated, making it clear it was the method she disapproved of, not the celebration.

"Yes. I—"

He held his breath as Bessy Lou took the book and examined the front cover, the back cover, flipped the pages to see if they'd fall out, held the book sideways and checked the list price. He supposed that all schoolteachers were like that, suspicious of everything until they knew what it meant. Even, he amended, a schoolteacher who was also a part-time seamstress for the rich folks on the hill. Or, in this case, the rich folks on the plantation. Which might as well have been on a hill for all the social climbing it took to get an invitation inside.

"Roger, are you thinking again?"

Shamefaced, he lowered his head. "Sorry."

"No matter."

Then, miraculously, the anger faded from her face, though it left behind a blush on her cheeks and the tip of her nose that took his breath away. He did his best not to fidget when she opened the book to its first page.

"It's a novel," he said.

"They all are, Roger," she muttered without looking up.

He tipped his hat to a pair of elderly women passing by, glanced across the street to the brick-faced savings and loan where he had to deposit what was left of his latest royalty check before closing, flattened his tie with a palm, felt an almighty desire to sneeze.

"Stop fussing, Roger," Bessy Lou muttered.

"Sorry."

She looked up at last. "Is this one for me?"

Now he felt himself blushing. "If . . . if you want it."

The book rapped him playfully on the chest. "Now, don't I have all the others?" A giggle. "Of course I want this one." Another giggle. "Something to pass the time while I'm working at the Manor tonight."

"Damn," he said.

She frowned.

His smile was at once apologetic and rueful. "Sorry again, Bessy Lou, but I had been counting on asking you to have dinner with me this evening. At Chez Zilla." He pointed at the book. "Another part of the celebration. If you'll have me, that is. As a date, I mean," he added quickly.

When her expression changed to one of sincere regret, he felt another almighty urge, this one to grab her manfully by the arms, pull her close enough for a morals charge, and tell her exactly how he felt whenever he saw her, or thought about her, or dreamed of her, or thought about dreaming about her whenever he saw her. All this admiration from afar was a royal pain in the ass, and he was getting more than a little sick of having to play the bashful suitor. Unfortunately there was nothing he could do about it. Bessy Lou had seen some terrible tragedies in her young life, and he wasn't about to scare her away by coming on too strong.

"Wish I could, Rog."

"No problem. How about tomorrow?" Her smile was so angelic, he nearly fell back against the wall again. "Well, why not?" he continued expansively. "It's my book, right? I can celebrate any way and any time I want to."

She pressed the book to her breast. "Can you pick me up at seven?"

"Seven it is."

She looked up and down the street, leaned up and kissed him on the cheek, whispered in his ear, "You won't be sorry, Roger. I'll make it up to you." Then she hurried off, all parts of her swinging and swaying in several different directions without losing hold.

It took his breath away.

A quick prayer, a brief grin, and he strolled across the street to the bank. When he had completed his transaction, he knew that he had at last reached his goal—enough money to get the hell out of this goddamn town, buy a nice house and some land somewhere, and, if he was luckier than he'd ever been in his life, spend the rest of his days writing his books and taking care of Bessy Lou and her son, Timmy.

Tomorrow night he would find out. Tomorrow night, now that he knew he had the financial wherewithal to make good his escape, he was going to propose to her, flash the bankbook in her eyes, and dare her to refuse him.

Damn right, Rog, he told himself; damn right.

The train whistle turned his head.

The engine was coming into the station.

And a sudden chill made him roll his shoulders.

His left hand touched the bankbook in his pocket. None too soon, Roger, he thought as he hurried down the street toward the jewelry store; you're getting out of here none too soon.

Timmy Leigh grinned in delight when he heard the train's warning whistle as it left the arch of Howe's Bridge and thundered onto the flat that led into the station. He loved to feel the ground shake, watch the trees sway, see the birds lift in panic from the depths of the swamp and cloud the sky with their wings; he loved to race alongside the dusty cars as the train slowed for its stop, waving to the passengers, catching a few coins when he cartwheeled and such for their amusement; he dreamed every night of becoming an engineer and riding away on his trusty iron horse, even if it was a blunt-nosed diesel, away to the great cities of the Midwest and the West and maybe, if he was good, even the hellish North.

But not today.

Today was the most special day in his whole life after his birthday.

Today he, Timothy Leigh, was out for treasure.

So, reluctantly, he turned his back and poled his flat-bottom boat deeper into the bayou, skirting islands of tall sharp grass, winding around knees of cypress, and avoiding all the known nesting places of gators and cottonmouths.

The sun here was dappled but no less warm, and his thin cotton shirt stuck to his sweaty skin, while sweat trickled from his red hair, gathered on his freckles, darkened his knee-torn, rolled-up jeans. He wished he had brought some soda; the bayou water was too dank, too filled with *things* to be safe, and his throat was sand-dry and twice as coarse.

He also wished he hadn't come alone.

Not that he was afraid or anything. It was just that it would have been nice to have someone to talk to. On the other hand, if someone had come with him, he'd have to share the secret of the treasure, and he wasn't about to do that for anyone in the world except maybe his mother.

Mother.

Boy, was she ever going to be proud of him!

As soon as he rolled that big old treasure into the boat and brought it back to the house, she'd be able to sell it for millions of dollars. Zillions of dollars. And then . . . and then she would tell Mr. Howe to take a flying leap, and they'd be able to leave Howe's Landing forever. Never come back. Not even if Missy Briltine begged him; not even if she showed him for free what she showed all the other boys for a couple of bucks that he never had at one time anyway because he had to put it all in the bank to save for his college. Besides, his mother would tan his hide, blush his ass, cross his eyes with a baseball bat if she ever found out.

A mosquito landed on his arm.

He squished it with a thumb, wiped the blood off on his jeans, and steered the boat into a tunnel of Spanish moss and bare, twisted branches.

It wouldn't be long now.

Twenty minutes tops, and he'd be at the place he'd discovered last week.

The place of the treasure.

Timmy wasn't stupid. He knew that eggs were only a certain size because the mother that laid them was a certain size too. You get your big eggs because you got one big mother. And this mother must have been the size of Missouri. One look and he knew every scientist and teacher in the whole country would want to have it. And the only way they were gonna get it was to pay him and his mother a zillion dollars.

A splash to his right, and a red-banded snake coasted along the surface toward the pole. Timmy watched it carefully, and let go a held breath when the snake suddenly whipped around in the other direction.

He wiped sweat from his brow with a forearm.

Bubbles broke on the brown water with dull plops, gases rising from decaying vegetable matter long submerged, long forgotten; a bird called to him from high atop an island pine, and he answered with a practiced trilling of his own; something growled in a reed thicket off to his left; something muttered behind a thorn bush on a stretch of high dry ground where, it was said, Indians still lived, coming out only at night to scalp the idiots who plied the bayou under a full moon.

Finally he reached a solitary island whose sides were a good four feet high and covered with weeds. He tied the boat to a dead log and clambered ashore, using a stick he'd brought to swish in front of him to scare away snakes and deadly spiders.

There wasn't much here: a few lightning-blasted trees trying to come back, some low shrubs with wilting leaves, and, in the center, a mound of dirt as high as his head. He walked around it carefully, checking the ground for signs of intruders, then used a vine to climb to the top.

There, in the middle, was a nest.

Five feet across, three feet high. Made of branches, not twigs; mud, beer cans, an oar, and the skins of more dead critters than he could count.

And in the nest he could just make out the rounded top of the giant egg—pale blue, with a webbing of dark red.

He shook his fists in triumph, shouted silently, grinned at the sky already losing its sun. Then, from around his waist he unwrapped a huge burlap sack and a ten-foot length of rope. The best thing, he figured, was to climb inside and bag the egg first, tie it securely, then haul it gently but firmly back to the boat. It would just about fit, which was another reason why he hadn't taken anyone with him.

He licked his lips, dried his hands on his sides, approached the nest, and, using a stout length of log, lifted himself up.

And gaped.

"Oh," he said.

The egg was there all right.

Except that there was a hole in its side.

A large hole.

Hell, it was a huge hole.

And from the evidence of the shell shards lying below it, whatever had made that hole had come from the inside.

Timmy dropped to the ground and didn't think twice about racing back to his boat. If he could have gotten away with it, he would have run across the water; as it was, he had to content himself with poling his fool head off, praying and wishing and hoping and praying again that he'd make it back to Howe's Landing without getting lost.

He had to get his mother back out here before dark.

He had to get someone back out here before dark.

If he didn't get someone, anyone, back out here before dark, no one would believe him until it was too late that the stories were true.

All of them.

But especially the one about the monster they called gopher.

·2·

When the train pulled away from the depot a scant minute
after it had stopped, a lone passenger remained behind on the
platform, two well-traveled suitcases at his feet, hands clasped
loosely before him. He was tall without being overpowering,
muscularly lean, and handsome without being pretty about it.
A slightly squared jaw. Quiet ginger hair of such startling abundance that middle-aged men wanted to scalp him on the spot,
and women wanted to find out if it came off in the shower.
Grey-lensed sunglasses that masked his eyes, a tasteful pale
blue suit with unbuttoned jacket, and a faintly striped cream
shirt whose color-coordinated tie had long since been relegated
to the jacket's right front pocket.

Dapper without being foppish; elegant without being osten-
tatious; cool without being cold.

A bird cried overhead.

Crickets chirped in the shade.

A warm breeze eddied dust down through cracks in the
flooring.

The passenger nodded to himself, took a deep breath, and
marveled at the clarity and taste of the air, the commingling
aromas of a dozen sweet blossoms, the temperature which
was neither oppressive nor debilitating. Just hot. He noted

the delightful, albeit ominous, jungle-like tangle of tree and
brush and vibrant wildflower on the far side of the empty
tracks, and the gemlike sparkle of standing water beyond; he
saw how the sturdy rails running north and south were shiny
and worn by decades of steel wheels passing over them on their
way from one exotic destination to another; he was able to note
that the leaf-infested, willow-lined parking lot behind the station
house was evidently wide enough for a dozen automobiles, and
was empty and in need of serious repair; he could not help
but spot the deranged-looking pegleg scarecrow in coveralls
and bleached long-john top with sleeves rolled to the pointy
elbows, sitting in a chair and pointing an antique revolver at
his chest; he was not unaware that the two men standing near
the scarecrow were watching him warily, as if he had disem-
barked with an open vial of the world's most virulent
plague.

He looked around again.

Another deep breath, this one more in the immediate neigh-
borhood of a sigh.

I am, he thought at last, doomed.

A rather formidable-looking man, of near similar height and
considerably broader bulk, in a hideous green polyester suit with
black knit tie and braid-laden chauffeur's cap, pushed away from
the post he had been leaning against and sauntered over. His gaze
traveled from shoe to hat before he touched the bill of his cap
and said, "You the lordship guy?"

Doomed.

Kent Montana nodded. There was nothing else he could do.
It would have been bad form to scream, and rather difficult to
explain.

"It's okay, Silas," the chauffeur called laughingly over his
shoulder. "Ain't what you're looking for."

"Which is?" Kent asked as his suitcases were snatched up as
though they were empty.

"Just some local redneck superstition," the man answered
derisively as he clumped across the platform. "Ain't nothing
to worry about."

Of course not, Kent thought.

"Name's Joe Bill Spain."

Of course it is, Kent thought.

"Gonna be your driver long as you're hanging around this neck of the woods."

Of course you are, God bless you.

They passed the man with the wooden leg and the gun.

Doomed; lord, he was doomed.

Then, as long as he was doomed anyway, he stopped. He didn't really want to, but he couldn't help it. It had something to do with fate, inevitability, and the terminal curiosity of a man about to be awesomely stupid.

"Are you the local sheriff, sir?" he asked politely, relieved that the gun had sagged into the man's lap. This close, he would swear the fellow smelled like alligator shoes, except that he was wearing a particularly nasty mud-smeared boot on his good leg, with metal crescents nailed to the toe.

The man wrinkled his nose, spat to one side, wrinkled his nose again. "Nope. The Watcher."

"I see."

"Yep. Been watching for so long now, I can't remember when I started."

"Ah." He squinted against the bright sunlight as he scanned the platform, the tracks, the flora on the other side. Preferably for a hidden camera; failing that, a fast car with a full tank and keys waiting in the ignition; failing that, a merciful bolt of lightning.

"Yep. Three hundred a week for boring my ass off. Gotta do it, though. Can't never can tell, if you know what I mean."

Kent's nod was sage. "Escaped convicts, I assume? Madmen? Perhaps there is a prison or asylum located nearby?"

The man's eyes narrowed suspiciously. "What you want to know that for?"

"Hey," yelled Spain from the other end of the platform, "we gotta get going, mister."

Kent, sensing an inadvertent transgression of local custom, smiled his apology. "No offense, sir. Just curious, that's all." He turned the smile on the chubby man in the stationmaster's uniform. "One removes oneself from a train in an unfamiliar community, one doesn't normally expect to have a gun pointed at him, does one. You see."

The stationmaster nodded agreeably. "Yep. Can see why that might be a start, you being a stranger and all."

"Hey, damnit!"

"So . . ." Kent shrugged. "I wondered."

"One what?" the scarecrow demanded.

Kent cocked his head. "I'm sorry?"

"One what? You says one, and I says one what?"

"Oh. Well, in this case, one me, I suppose."

The stationmaster chuckled amiably as he gestured toward the otherwise deserted station. "He got you there, Silas. He's the one, but far as I can see, he ain't the one you're watching for. Not unless that one's gonna be wearing hundred-dollar suits and stuff."

"I sincerely hope not," Kent said. The gun was still in Silas's lap, but now its muzzle was aimed at a muscular but vulnerable leg.

"Rudy Humpquin," the stationmaster said cordially, offering a hand.

Kent took it, shook it firmly. "Montana," he said.

"Never been there," Silas muttered.

"Guess you're here for the big do up at the Manor?"

Kent eyed the revolver when the scarecrow crossed his legs, a movement which automatically elevated the trajectory. He hesitated, uncertain. Was this a trick question? If he answered incorrectly, would he ever have children? If it was only a flesh wound, would he be able to get home to his modest but thriving estate on an unnamed scenic Hebrides isle and spend the rest of his days in reasonable peace, tending his grapes and wenching the neighbors the way any self-respecting peer of the realm would, if he had neighbors?

"Aye," he answered cautiously, tense and ready to leap to safety.

Humpquin blinked. "I see. It ought to be something. Them parties always are." He fussed with a pocket watch, opening and closing its lid. "I, uh, noticed that Joe Bill there, he called you a lordship a while back."

"You coming, you moving in, for god's sake?" Spain yelled in exasperation, dropping the suitcases and planting his hands on his hips.

"That's right," Kent said. "Baron, actually."

"Oil?"

"Title."

Humpquin looked confused. "No offense, Baron, but you talk kinda funny. You ain't from around here, right?"

"Not so's you'd notice, no."

"Thought so. Got an ear for them things."

"Yes," Kent agreed. "And a good one it is, too." He touched his brow in friendly farewell and backed away. "Well, thank you both, gentlemen, for your generous time, and I do hope you find whatever it is you're watching for."

At that, the stationmaster took a step back, gulped and paled, his hands fluttering uncontrollably to his suddenly fluttering lips.

"Jesus Christ, man!" Silas snapped, uncrossing his legs and waving the gun wildly. "My God, watch what you're saying!"

Before Kent could respond, or duck, Spain grabbed his elbow and pulled him away.

"What the hell'd you want to go and say something like that for?" the man stage-whispered fearfully.

"Say what? I was only being polite." He pulled his arm free and dusted the offended cloth. "He was pointing that weapon at me, remember?"

"Well, hell, I saw that. Jesus, what'd you expect him to do? Come right up to you, say 'Hey, you the one I gotta blow away afore this town gets tromped into blood and bone and ain't never heard of again'?" He shook his head in utter disgust. "Christ, you foreigners, you're all alike."

Kent paused before following him down the steps and into the side lot, wondering precisely how much would be considered enough before United States law permitted him to embark upon a thoroughly justified yokel euthanasia spree. It was bad enough all these people had accents he could barely understand; it was bad enough this hole-in-the-swamp town wasn't New Orleans, Baton Rouge, or even the outskirts of Shreveport; it was bad enough his back and butt ached from that miserable four-hour train ride on what had to have been a stone seat cleverly disguised as cracked imitation leather.

Did he, dear Lord, have to put up with mystery and intrigue as well?

He didn't know.

Probably.

But it wasn't exactly the way he had planned to spend his weekend in the Old South. That particular dream, which had so

devoutly sustained him ever since he had left London four days
ago, contained things more along the lines of an abundance of
sumptuous Southern cooking, lovely (and sumptuous) Southern
women, intelligent and totally meaningless conversations over
expensive brandy in the library, semitropical nights under the
Southern stars—and some time to himself in order to devise a
way to reverse the downward direction his acting career had tak-
en since he'd been fired from his longstanding role as an erudite
English butler on the continuing daytime drama *Passions and
Power*.

In the meantime, his agent had promised faithfully to be in
touch before the weekend was over, swearing on his mother's
undug grave that a truly magnificent, profitable, and stellar deal
was in the works, which he was not at liberty to discuss but
would probably set Kent up for life.

Unfortunately, being set up for life was not his problem.

He already was set up for life. As long, that is, as his mother
continued to be as inept in her assassination attempts as she had
been in the past. Clever, however; he did have to give her that—
she was clever.

Money, therefore, was not one of his more pressing prob-
lems.

What he wanted, what he needed, what he had to damnit have,
was work. Acting work. Performing for his fans. Treading the
boards, filling the silver screen, emoting, reacting, and generally disproving the theory that a genuine Scots baron couldn't
dramatize his way out of a paper kilt.

The inactivity was driving him nuts.

But he wasn't so nuts that mystery and intrigue would be a
welcome addition to his physical and psychological baggage.
Nuts was not the same as crazy.

A casual glance over his shoulder: the stationmaster was
watching him and smiling; the scarecrow was watching him
and scratching his wooden leg with the gun.

Kent, his agent had said, *this dude's rich, he's looking for
an actor; he's impressed as hell about your title, and he wants
to look you over for a film he's thinking of producing. What the
hell, it's a free trip, right, babe? Who knows? This could be the
start of something big.*

Look me over, Kent thought.

Mr. Howe's expecting me, Kent thought.

There'll probably be a bathing suit competition.

His temper sparked, one fist clenched, and he wondered just who in the hell this mysterious Mr. Howe thought he was.

The chauffeur looked at him. "You finished?"

Kent looked back.

The chauffeur opened the back door. "All this jawing and thinking and stuff, we're gonna be late. Mr. Howe'll skin me alive."

"I shall accept full responsibility."

"Damn right," the man grumbled. He took off his cap, scratched through his hair, replaced the cap with a determined yank on the bill and guided him into the backseat. "What the hell, I can always mulch in the morning. Be too hot by the time we get there, anyway."

"Mulch?"

Another look, and a scowl at the two men on the platform who, if they moved any closer, would have fallen off.

"My roses," the chauffeur said in a way that dared him to laugh.

Which Kent didn't though he suspected his expression was one of mild astonishment that a man of this size, in that godawful suit, actually grew roses.

The chauffeur closed the door, took his place behind the wheel, and drove out of the parking lot, braked at the exit, looked into the rearview mirror, and said, "I ain't gonna call you Lord or nothing, y'know."

"That's fine with me," Kent assured him.

"Wouldn't be right. This here is America, case you forgot. We're all equal in this country. We don't got no damn lords and stuff like that here." The car eased forward. "I'll call you Mr. Montana, it ain't polite to say 'hey you.' But I sure as hell ain't gonna bow or nothing. People around here, they don't take to crap like that. The U.S. Constitution, it doesn't say nothing about bowing. And man, you try that here in Louisiana, you get your nose clipped off sure as you sneeze first thing in the morning. *Mr.* Montana. That's as far as I go."

Kent opened his mouth to assure the chauffeur that bowing, and a little obsequious scraping, while not entirely unpleasant in their place, were also not required. Not by him, at any rate, and certainly not for short-tempered men who obviously weighed in excess of fifteen stone and bulged their jackets to the point of torture. But he changed his mind. That would surely bring about another sullen monologue, and he did not want anything to spoil this moment.

Instead, he concentrated on the view as the automobile turned left and drifted past several wooded lots, and beyond them a half-dozen houses not in the best of condition. A yellowish mongrel trotted beside them in the gutter until a squirrel across the way drew it into a barking chase. A crow pecked at something on the blacktop. He began to feel ashamed for his earlier presentiment of doom.

When they reached the intersection, and he saw the houses, the signs and shops, a few giggling children rolling a hoop along the sidewalk, cars parked at the curb, ladies with shopping bags hooked over their arms, he chastised himself thoroughly.

Howe's Landing was not a backwater town at all.

It was just small. And unhurried. And definitely not worthy of his well-honed sense of paranoia.

"Lovely. It's really quite lovely."

"Stop," said Kent.

Spain did. "What?"

Kent peered through his window, then opened his door and stepped out.

"Hey, damnit!"

The shop that had caught his attention was, like most of the others, fronted by white clapboard, and in its window was displayed on soft dark blue cloth the most incredible array of doilies, antimacassars, and lace shawls he had ever seen outside Brussels. They were exquisite. They were delicate. They were so intricate that he had to look away for a moment after trying to follow one of the patterns. Though no prices were marked, a hand-lettered sign guaranteed the potential buyer that the goods offered here, and inside, were handmade from materials grown on local farms.

"Lady stuff," Spain muttered over his shoulder; he wasn't impressed.

There was also a poster tucked in the window's left-hand corner, the same one he'd seen in several other stores but hadn't been able to read. It was bright red on bright yellow and said simply: STOP THE BAYOU BLAST SAVE THE GATORS. When asked, the chauffeur was reluctant to explain, and Kent didn't push it, supposing that even here, in remote Humbert Parish, a developer wanted to do something with some land, and the people didn't want him to do it. Oh hell; that meant he would soon be faced with greed, connivance, and feigned loyalties on top of all the mystery and intrigue.

He just wished he could figure out what his part in all this was. Not for a minute had he really believed that bull his agent had handed him about a rich producer looking for royal talent. A couple of hours, maybe, but not one minute longer.

"C'mon, c'mon," Spain prodded. "Time's running out, you want me to lose my job?"

But Kent only moved to the next store along, a florist in whose window was a sign, bright yellow on bright red, that said, simply: BUILD THE BAYOU BLAST, GATORS CAN'T VOTE. Of course, he thought, and would have returned instantly to the car had he not noticed a single gold rose in a milk-white vase. A tiny card at the base named it "Spain Dawn."

He smiled faintly. "Coincidence?"

The chauffeur snarled wordlessly.

"It's . . . extraordinary."

The chauffeur scuffed his shoe on the pavement.

"I take it this is your work?"

A brief vacillation before the man suddenly smiled, a startling smile that actually made him appear human. "I got this great place out on the Manor," he said enthusiastically, quietly, a hand lightly pressed against the pane. "I got a rose there, you can't grow it nowhere else in the state." His chest puffed. "Four firsts at the State Fair, four years in a row."

"Congratulations," Kent said sincerely. What the hell; roses were better than guard dogs.

"Yeah, well . . . thanks."

Kent smiled a *don't mention it shall we go* and returned to the Mercury. Once inside, Spain took the wheel, hesitated, and twisted around in his seat. "Y'know," he said, though obviously discomfited, "you got some free time later, I'd be pleased maybe you could drop by my place, maybe, I don't know, you being a lord and all, maybe you'd like a drink or something without folks hanging all over you, which they're gonna do. You being a lord and all."

Kent scratched two fingers lightly down his throat, considered the heat now and what it was likely to be later, and decided that this curious man just might be good to have on his side. Whichever side that was. As soon as he knew what was going on. "I think something like that just might be in order, Mr. Spain. Yes. Thank you."

The chauffeur grinned and faced front, released the brake and drove on. "Okay. Ain't gonna be great drinking, of course, but I got a scotch last time I was in New Orleans make your ears grow fur." One eye half closed. "You like scotch?"

"I've been known," Kent replied.

Spain froze for a moment, mouth open, eyes glazed. "Oh," he said at last. "Yeah. Forgot. You're Scotch."

"Scots," Kent corrected gently. "Scotch is what you have in that bottle of yours." A bit of deliberation himself. Then: "Perhaps, if you'd like, you would try a little something I have in my luggage. A little something I brought from home."

Spain's eyes widened. "Really?"

"Glenbannock."

The car lurched forward. "You're shitting me."

Kent leaned back in amazement. "You've heard of it?"

"Are you kidding, man? That's . . . that's . . ." His voice lowered to a reverent whisper. "In . . . your gear?"

"My private stock," Kent told him.

Spain gasped. "Yours? Private? *Yours*?"

This, Kent thought, is getting out of hand.

He reached out and tapped the man's shoulder. "Drive on, Mr. Spain, drive on. As you say, we don't have much time."

"Stop."

"Again?"

"Then just drive more slowly, if you please."

"I drive any slower, a damn turtle can beat us to the Day of Judgment. What now?"

Kent pointed to a bar whose sign identified it as Della Depew's. A woman swept the sidewalk in front of it.

"That," he said.

"Della Depew."

"Yes, Mr. Spain, I can read." The car slipped past; the woman looked up, puzzled. "But who is that?"

"Della Depew."

Kent looked out the back window. "She's the owner?"

Spain chuckled. "You could say that."

"She's the owner."

"You got it."

Kent smiled. "A lovely woman."

Spain laughed. "Guess she is, but you'd better not say anything like that to Mr. Howe."

The smile was replaced by a frown. "Jilted lover, I suppose? Or a poor relation of the plantation aristocracy? Or the wife of someone who works at the Manor, who's compromising his principles on behalf of some nefarious scheme, which leaves her torn between her own principles and her love for her man?"

"You watch soap operas or something?"

"Daytime dramas," he corrected stiffly.

The Mercury began to gain speed. "Don't matter. You just don't want to get mixed up with her."

"A trollop?"

"She's a nurse."

"She owns the bar?"

"Comes in handy."

"I suppose. But what makes you think I wouldn't want to get to know her better?"

Spain tromped on the accelerator. "Baron, there's things going on around here you don't know about."

"Tell me about it," he muttered.

"Ain't my place to. But that lady there, she's the reason the Bayou Blast ain't gonna get built in my lifetime."

Greed. Intrigue. Factions. Town divided by loyalty and monetary persuasion. Brother against brother. Sister against sister. Families torn asunder.

"Mr. Spain, when does the next train leave?"

"Monday morning, if he bothers to stop."

"I see."

Spain glanced at him in the rearview mirror. "Baron, no offense, but I think you picked yourself one dumbass time to come to Howe's Landing."

· 3 ·

Blanche Knox sat at her hand-wrought, brass-studded mahogany desk, opened her rich Corinthian leather appointment book to today's date, and trailed a perfectly manicured finger down the page. Her vivid red lips smiled; her sultry green eyes brightened; her other hand picked up a gold Cross pen and tapped a cheery message on the top of a Steuben glass penguin-on-an-ice-floe paperweight she generally used to flatten out wrinkled dollar bills.

The page was empty.

There would be no sick people coming to the Howe Clinic today.

Thank heaven.

She picked up her genuine white-and-gold Louis IX telephone and dialed while she closed the book, dusted it with a scented tissue, and dropped the tissue into an elephant's foot wastebasket.

"Morning, you great big swamp stud you," she said a moment later. "I've got good news for you."

Her answer was a muffled groan.

"Oh you!" She giggled, pursed her lips, and blew a wet, loud, prolonged kiss into the mouthpiece. "You're just saying that."

The groan became a sigh.

"Hey," she said, lowering her voice and cupping her palm around her chin while she gazed out the huge plate-glass window that overlooked the clinic's front yard and the park, "I'm not going to be busy today, sugar. Nobody's in the book, and I saw Doc knocking a few down in the barbershop. You want to come over and get examined?"

The groaning stopped.

The sighing stopped.

Blanche idly fingered the mother-of-pearl buttons of her white uniform blouse. Though the outfit was mandatory with the position, she hated wearing white. It did nothing for her extravagantly curly blonde hair or her delicately pale skin. On the other hand, its cut and fit did wonders for her figure, which more than once had driven Pruit gasping to the blood pressure apparatus.

"Honeybun, you listening?"

A gasp.

She nodded, and lowered her voice even more. "I found something in his office yesterday."

Expectant silence.

"Seems like the randy old bastard's been writing his memoirs on the sly."

A questioning grunt.

"Think you'll be mighty interested in what he has to say about what went on here a few years back." She wriggled in her chair, settled, took a cigarette from an engraved silver-and-ebony case and lit it with an engraved gold-and-emerald lighter. "Before I was born, of course."

The voice on the other end tickled her ear.

"Well, naturally I didn't tell anyone, you silly bear. You're the only one I'd breathe a word to, you know that, sweet sugar pie."

The voice buzzed, and she closed her eyes slowly.

"Darling, you get your organs over here in fifteen minutes, I'll show you pages you ain't never thought you'd see in your whole life! And," she added with a waggle of her superbly plucked eyebrows, "I learned a thing or two about that little rubber hammer too."

The grunt again.

Her eyelids fluttered. "Oh now, you just hold your little

horses, you hefty muskrat ramble you. You get here, that'll be soon enough." She kissed at the mouthpiece again. "Hurry, darling." Her voice dropped to a husky whisper. "My white shoes are off."

She hung up, and fanned herself with both hands. "My my," she said. "I do go on, don't I?"

Then she eased her high-backed leather wing chair away from the desk and padded across the thick Persian carpet to the window, the better to get a look at the road crew taking a break in the park by playing a game of touch football. They were shirtless, sweating, tanned, young, and altogether too delicious for words. So she whistled at them, laughed because they couldn't hear her, and turned around, trying to decide what to do until her favorite gator wrestler arrived.

Admittedly, being the full-time Howe Clinic receptionist didn't require a great deal of creativity unless it involved figuring out how some of these people spelled their last names and the disgusting diseases they had; and she certainly hadn't had a lot of work to do since Doc had hired her last year straight out of beautician school, though that was less his fault than the fact that the whole town wasn't more than five, six hundred people on a good day and the horses weren't running in Arkansas; and the days did get kind of long and lonely when there wasn't anybody to talk to but yourself and that giant of a Cajun janitor, Henry Fleuret, who never once to her knowledge even tried to get a peek at her cleavage so she could complain and get his unappreciative half-breed ass fired.

However, there were compensations.

Such as the personally decorated office she now stood in; such as the many interesting things she had come to learn about some of the important people in this town; such as not having to see a lot of blood and guts and oozing rashes because there was a nurse for all that icky stuff, even if the nurse did run a bar; such as her ever-expanding and increasingly healthy bank account, which was augmented on more than one occasion by those generous gentlemen callers who preferred to lavish gifts upon her in ways they had never imagined possible in a place like this with a woman like her.

But enough of this, she thought; time to get ready for that simply darling potent possum of hers.

From her cleavage she pulled a small cotton bag, out of which she took a small silver key she used to unlock the bottom drawer of her desk, out of which she took a thick sheath of papers held together by a desperate rubber band. Photocopies, not the originals, of what she had found in Doc's private safe, which he thought was successfully hidden behind the liquor cabinet in the emergency operating room.

Nothing in the clinic was hidden from Blanche Knox.

Not even the emergency operating room liquor cabinet artfully disguised as an instrument sterilization unit. Hell, she'd discovered that the first day she was here.

Carefully, then, she placed the pile on the desk and stared thoughtfully at it. Although she had skimmed through most of it, she barely understood what she had read. A lot of technical talk, doctor stuff and science stuff, and tons and tons of things underlined in red with bold exclamation points next to them. It made her cross-eyed just thinking about it. It also made her a little uneasy, because there were also parts that she did understand without having to use the dictionary, parts that talked a lot about gruesome deaths and inexplicable disappearances and lord almighty, that man did go on. And on. Until she had had a revelation: this stuff was worth considerably more than the paper it was printed on.

This stuff could make her one very rich woman.

Just thinking about it made her pant; just imagining all that money she could run barefoot through if she wanted to made her whole body tingle; just thinking about all that panting and tingling made her leap to her feet and head for the water cooler in the hall, where she drank four cups before she was able to breathe normally again.

Lord, she thought.

"Lordy," she whispered.

If this was what being rich and powerful did to you, no wonder the Howes had so many kids.

The front door opened.

She turned to tell the sick and disgusting person that the doctor was not in, wasn't expected in, and don't you dare tramp that mud on my brand new Persian rug.

It wasn't a patient.

"Oh my," she said breathlessly. "Oh my."

• • •

The mayor's two-room-if-you-didn't-count-the-back-stairs
office was over the savings and loan. The mayor, who also happened to be founder and president of the savings and loan, had
been in his chair, staring down at his tranquil domain, when he
happened to spot that idiot, Joe Bill Spain, park in the middle of
the street to let a pansy in a pale blue suit out of the Howe Manor
Mercury. They hung around a couple of shops, exchanged a few
words the mayor's binoculars and lip-reading abilities couldn't
catch, and returned to the car.

"Thury!" he called.

His door was open.

"What?"

"Thury, who's the fruit Spain's holding hands with?"

"Rude says he came in on the train," his secretary yelled back.
"Going up the Manor, supposed to be. Rude says he's some kind
of lord."

"Jesus, a minister?"

"No! One of those English guys. You know, the queen and
duke and like that?"

Queen, thought the mayor, is right.

On the other hand, the mayor didn't much care if the guy
was a Northern liberal lawyer with a black wife and fourteen
Chinese children; if he had been invited to the Manor, he was
someone he ought to know.

And if the fruit had been invited to the Manor, why hadn't
he been told about it? Was ol' Montague holding something
out on him? Unless, of course, it wasn't anything more than
a surprise to be sprung on him once he showed up, and there
was nothing to worry about at all. Unless the surprise was that
the fruit was going to take his place in the scheme of things.
Which, he thought, wasn't very likely, since he, the ever-elected
Stonewall Weatherly, knew so much about what was going on
around here that Montague didn't dare try to ace him out of
the picture. Unless, of course, the fruit was a hired killer from
Nevada. Which he doubted, because Howe had his own ways
of taking care of people he didn't much care for, thank you and
have a good day, so what the hell was going on?

Mercy, this job was hard sometimes.

"Rich!" Thury yelled.

"What?"

"Rich! He's rich! Rude figures him for one of those Blast men. Looking the place over."

The mayor grinned.

Now that made more sense.

Of course.

Unless—

He rubbed his hands, scrubbed his cheeks, used the flat of his palm to flatten his hair, and pushed himself out of his chair. "Think maybe I'll head out that way, see what's happening. Maybe talk to the guy myself."

"You'll meet him tonight," she bellowed.

"Yeah, but it doesn't hurt to get a leg up, does it? Lord, you say?"

"Baron, Rude says!"

"Oil?"

"How the hell should I know?"

The outer office telephone rang.

The mayor shrugged into his white suit jacket, picked up his white straw fedora with the red paisley band, and once again flattened his hair with a palm. He considered giving Wally Torn a call, and shook his head. The sheriff, blast his ass, was no ally. Not yet. Damn man actually thought he was independent, could run the town on his own. Lawmen damn sure got the dumbest ideas sometimes.

"Mayor!" the secretary yelled.

"What!" Damn. One of these days he was going to get himself an intercom. To hell with the budget.

"Bessy Leigh!"

"What about her?" Except that she was the best thing this town ever saw in a skirt, and God bless those youngsters for having her all to themselves every day.

"Says her Timmy saw the gopher!"

"What!"

"The gopher!"

"Jesus Christ, don't yell!"

He rushed into the outer office and stared at his secretary, the closest thing he could find to a Blanche Knox of his own, which wasn't very close.

"My god, Thury," he whispered.

Thury shrugged. "He's only a tad, Mayor. What's he know about—"

"Hush!"

Thury glanced suspiciously around the empty office. "He's only a tad," she repeated.

"Yes," he said ominously, "but tads talk to other tads who talk to their mommas like this tad done. We get something like this going around town, not only do we get Silas plugging everyone who looks like . . . well, you know . . . but we get nervous investors who just might wonder whether we're good enough for their money."

Thury blew on her nails. "Guess you better get to that baron fella, then, hadn't you? Let him know it's all a joke."

The mayor nodded, squared his shoulders, told her he'd be back before long, hold all his calls. But as soon as he was in the stairwell, his shoulders sagged and his breath came hard. Tads talk. Mommas talk. Lord in a willow, he hoped Montague wouldn't hear. Last thing the man said to him, not three nights ago, was that everything was delicate now, we don't want these men spooked, so keep people like Myrtle Mae and Silas as far away from them as you can.

That part was easy.

But tads talk.

And when they do, money walks.

"Silas?"

"Yeah, Rude?"

"You could've killed that lord guy, y'know."

"Well, he ain't got a right talking stuff like that while I'm doing my watching."

Rudy moved closer. "He didn't know."

Silas scowled at the tracks. "Maybe he didn't, maybe he did."

"C'mon, Silas, you can't mean that."

"Maybe I do, maybe I don't."

Rudy moved closer still. "Jesus, Silas, the man's from a foreign country, he can't know nothing lest something already told him, which they didn't, otherwise he would've stayed on that train and gone on to Minneapolis."

"Well . . . maybe he didn't, and maybe he didn't."

Rudy didn't respond. He hated it when Silas got himself all mysterious and enigmatic like that. Man weren't fit to live with, talking in riddles, refusing to take a position, spitting all over the platform trying to hit the lizards. Made another man sometimes want to take a saw to his damn leg.

"Rude?"

"What."

"You're standing on my foot."

Not far from town, there was an island in the bayou. It was large enough for several three-room single-story shacks on sturdy stilts, a motley collection of outbuildings, a few rusted hulks of automobiles, and a chicken coop fashioned out of linoleum strips and driftwood, some of which had made it all the way up from the Gulf. Profuse natural vegetation and quite a large successful garden filled in the rest. It was connected to the mainland by a narrow, twenty-foot-long footbridge built from saplings, rope, and planks scrounged from construction sites around the parish; strong enough for a man, not nearly strong enough for a pickup or car—those that worked were parked in a clearing on the other side.

And in the bed of one of those trucks, sitting on a pile of empty burlap sacks, Jacques Fleuret whittled as he waited for his father to return from town with the weekend supplies. He had volunteered to go in with him, but had been ordered to stick close to home.

Something was in the air.

Something bad.

"Like what?" Jacques had asked.

"Don't know, son. You just stay where you are. Keep your eyes open. Listen. Watch. Pay attention. Stay awake. You see something funny, you hear something funny, you even smell something funny you know is not right, you get your family inside. You don't look around, you don't try to be the hero. You just get them inside, bolt the doors and windows, keep your filthy hands off your cousin Louisa."

Jacques, who generally thought his father was a little tilted, had shivered then, despite the fact that they had been standing in a patch of hot sunlight. And then—*mon Dieu!*—he had been given part of the family arsenal—a twelve-gauge double-barrel

Remington with an eagle carved in the stock, last used to pepper Silas Bouquette's ass for reasons nobody could now remember.

That scared him.

So he whittled. And he whistled. Chewed on a blade of grass. Tilted his head when he heard the distant voice of the train, and wished for a moment that he could be there to see it. He loved trains. All his life he had never been on one; at night, when he wasn't dreaming about his cousin Louisa, he dreamt about the trains.

Someday, he vowed to himself for the hundredth time, he was going to take one to someplace, it didn't matter where; and when he got back—

A shriek of laughter, and he shook the reverie away, remembering his assignment, though he still didn't know why he had it.

He supposed, however, it was better than being over there on the island, where his sister, his uncle Pier, and cousin Louisa were putting a second coat of bright red paint on the main house and its stilts. It looked dumb. It looked like a firehouse. It was so bright, he knew he'd be able to see it in the middle of the night without a lamp. It scared the possums away. It got the raccoons so angry they threw crawdads at the porch. But the paint had been free, and the labor was free, and his father had reminded them that the place hadn't been done over since 1964 and maybe it was about time to bring the homestead into the contemporary world. After all, the kids would be the first Fleurets to graduate from high school, Momma had a chef's job at the Manor, and the old man himself was custodial engineer and maintenance supervisor at the prestigious Howe Clinic. Did they, he demanded when they howled their protests, want to live in a dingy hovel all their lives? Didn't they want to be proud of their heritage and not be ashamed to bring friends home for dinner? Weren't they tired of the same damn weathered brown all the time?

No one had disagreed.

No one dared. Poppa was six-and-a-half feet tall, weighed two hundred and forty pounds, and had once thrown an entire outhouse into the water when Uncle Pier, who had been inside at the time, had admitted to having an affair with Miz Beauregard's black cleaning lady, who was, at the time, old enough to be Uncle Pier's wife, for god's sake, what the hell kind of mistress was that for a man of forty-three?

So they painted.

And Jacques whittled and whistled and watched.

And suddenly jumped up in the truck and stared at the water running lazily under the bridge.

Something was floating or swimming in there, just below the surface.

Something large.

The way it was moving wasn't natural at all.

Without taking his gaze away, he picked up the shotgun and carefully climbed down to the ground. When he could catch no one's eye on the island, he crouched down and made his way across the bare earth to the bank, parted the reeds, and brought the shotgun quickly to his shoulder.

It was gone.

He smiled a little foolishly.

The smile became a grimace, and he swallowed when he heard a light thump under the bridge.

It wasn't gone.

Again no one saw him from the island, and he moved swiftly but silently to the other side, readied himself and slipped down the bank, almost to the water's edge.

This time he saw it and nearly lost his lunch.

It was a huge alligator, the biggest he'd seen in years—fat, a good fifteen, maybe twenty feet long, and floating on its back. It had no head. Its tail had been split in half. And its stomach was mutilated by dozens of deep gashes.

Something funny; something bad.

"Jonelle!" he yelled, leaping off the bank and waving his free arm. "Uncle Pier! Louisa! Come quick!"

Immediately the cry was given, Pier Granlieu threw down his brush and ordered the startled girls to stay where they were. He picked up a well-honed machete and hurried down to the bank. He looked where Jacques pointed. Puffed his bearded cheeks and shook his head slowly.

"What do you think?" Jacques said.

"Looks dead," his uncle replied gruffly. "Pretty dead, I'd say."

"Damnit," the boy yelled, "it's more than dead, it's sushi! And Poppa said we barricade ourselves inside right away if we saw something like this."

The girls came up to their uncle, jeans and T-shirts splattered red enough for the movies, long black hair tied in ponytails, faces flushed from their exertions. They took one look at the mutilated alligator and ran for the house, claiming first dibs on the rifle.

"Guess we're taking a break," Pier said.

Jacques looked around him, at the familiar trees both on land and growing out of the water, at the hillocks and hummocks, the bracken and the moss. He knew every inch of this bayou for miles around. And now, suddenly, he didn't know it at all.

◆ 4 ◆

The front doors of Howe Manor were solid teak, paneled, edged with iron bands. They were strong enough to withstand the entire Union army, hurricanes, and every other disaster known to man.

That man stood in front of them now.

He was tall, slender, slightly stooped, well-tanned, dressed entirely in white from his snug riding boots to a low-crowned hat whose floppy brim hid his face in dusky shadow. As he listened to a mockingbird sing in a nearby tree, he slapped his leg lightly with a white riding crop. Nodded. Looked down at the panting mastiff lying at his feet and said quietly, "Thor, I wonder what Joe Bill has done with our company." A deep voice, resonant, hinting of cruelty and laughter, sadism and sermons and Tennessee Williams, fairly dripping with an aristocratic Louisiana drawl.

The mastiff, of a color that reminded one of road kill too long in the sun, snorted and flapped its scarred ears.

One of the doors opened silently behind him.

"Daddy, did I hear the train a while back?"

"You certainly did, darlin'," he answered without turning around.

"Who went to meet it?"

"Joe Bill."

"Oh shoot."

"Now don't worry, sweetheart, he won't kill nobody unless I tell him."

"If you say so, Daddy."

"I sure do, sweetheart."

"He has a temper, Joe Bill does."

"He does, I agree. But I do believe he understands that we desire subtlety this time."

"Okay, Daddy. If you're sure."

"I'm sure, Peaches. Now, you run along and get things over and done, you hear? We only have a few hours before the first guests start arriving, and we don't want to be inhospitable. And Peaches? Darlin', do be sure your sister is taking care of Mrs. Fleuret and the kitchen, will you? You know how that woman gets when we're going to have a party."

"I do, Daddy, I surely do."

He smiled.

"Daddy?"

"Yes, darlin'."

"I don't mean to pester, truly I don't, but . . . well, do you think it's going to work this time? I mean, Granddaddy really blew it, you know. You think it'll be right this time?"

"Darlin', trust me. I've been over it a hundred times, awake and asleep. This time the Howes are going to make history. I guarantee it."

The door closed.

The man tapped Thor with his crop, and the beast lumbered noisily to its feet. "A short walk," he said gently, and strolled around the house, keeping to the veranda until he reached the back. There, he looked out over three acres of splendid back-yard dotted with several island gardens in full bloom, and white tables with matching chairs beneath huge rainbow umbrellas. A fountain at dead center. A quartet of peacocks strutting across the grass.

Thor huffed at the birds.

The man calmed him with a touch and headed directly toward the trees that marked the end of his land, the beginning of the western bayou. The dog trotted loyally beside him.

The breeze died.

The sun grew warmer.

Mosquitoes buzzed, gnats swarmed, truly ugly little things squirmed and rustled in the grass.

At the back a crumbling fieldstone wall was broken only by a stout iron gate with a new padlock and chain wrapped tightly through the bars. After checking to be sure no one was watching, the man took out a key, opened the padlock, drew the chain through the bars, opened the gate, let the mastiff go through first before following, closing the gate, arranging the chain, and locking the padlock. Beyond was a narrow dirt path interrupted every score of yards by narrow wooden bridges that allowed him to cross over the brackish water below.

Thor grunted once.

"Don't you worry," the man said, patting the beast's great head. "We'll be back in plenty of time. Plenty of time." And he laughed so loudly that the birds screamed into flight, a hissing cottonmouth bolted for cover, and several strands of Spanish moss withered and dropped into the water.

Oh yes, he thought gleefully; plenty of time indeed.

~ II ~

Howe's Manor

· 1 ·

The highway that led into Howe's Landing and, through no fault
of its own, momentarily became its main street, had only one
turnoff before it continued on its way to the neighboring parish. And once that turn was made, the road quickly narrowed
to barely the width of two healthy automobiles, and buildings
and yards were quickly replaced by carefully tended fields of
sugar cane and cotton and green leafy things and a couple of
purple-looking short things off in the hazy distance. In time
the fields became overgrown, then vanished altogether as the
elemental and primordial mix of forest and swamp reclaimed
the land. Mist rose in ghostly patches no matter the time of
day; daylight became twilight, and sunlight was tinted a faint
green, a fainter grey; invisible birds squawked, invisible wings
beat, bobcats yowled and alligators grunted, and every so often
Kent heard the angry cry of a hungry panther.

It reminded him of his mother the day she found out the
chocolate Valentine's bomb she'd sent him in Edinburgh hadn't
worked. And he wondered then if she had had anything to do with
bringing him here. It would be just like her. Save her the expense
of sending the assassins after him but still manage to get hold of the
baronial estate once he had been sent to that great proscenium in
the sky. Plus, she wouldn't have to clean up afterward.

"Tell me about Mr. Howe," he asked when all that Nature began to give him the willies.

"He's a bastard," Spain replied.

Kent closed his eyes. "Did you know he was thinking of making a movie?"

Spain laughed.

And three lonely miles later, the road slipped timidly into a long shady tunnel created by ancient red oaks whose massive crowns were intertwined, and whose thicker branches were scarred by the talons of patient buzzards.

"Tell me again, Mr. Spain. About Mr. Howe."

The chauffeur hunched his shoulders and cleared his throat nervously. "Well, sir, don't know that I ought to. I don't want to be going against the boss, y'know, he wouldn't like it much, got a temper he does. Why, the last time he got ticked at me he—"

Kent shifted, opened his eyes, caught the man looking at him in the rearview mirror, and smiled. Coldly.

Spain cleared his throat again. "Well, sir, first thing is, his wife is dead. Long time ago, before I come here to drive, so I can't tell you why, just that it's been a long time. There's two kind of young daughters, they kind of run things when he's busy, if you know what I mean. Then—"

"What, exactly, does Mr. Howe do?"

"He makes money."

Kent sat up. "A counterfeiter?"

"Baron, you deliberately dense or what?" the chauffeur asked, and shook his head. "I mean, he's rich. Richer'n God. Plants, gambles, land deals, all kinds of shit like that. Does stuff in his place out back I wouldn't want to guess, don't let nobody in there but Bambi."

Kent blinked slowly, once. "Bambi?"

"One of them two daughters I believe I mentioned a while ago."

Bambi. Kent had never been able to understand why one human being would name another human being Bambi. Even his mother wasn't that cruel.

"Bambi is a male," he said.

"Not so's you'd notice," Spain replied.

"No. In the movie of the same name. Bambi is a male. Prince of the Forest. Yet you Americans—"

"Hey, watch it!"

"—give the name to your women." He lifted a hand. "It's amusing, is it not?"

The chauffeur sneered.

Kent shrugged.

The chauffeur said, "Then, of course, there's that legend."

God, if You're there, Kent prayed, please strike this man dead without crashing the car.

"What legend?"

The chauffeur's eyes widened. "Didn't nobody tell you about the legend that's stuck to Howe Manor since practically before the beginning of time?"

"No. I was not told about a legend."

"Oh."

Kent waited.

Spain drove.

The swamp crowded the road.

"You wanna hear it?"

"No."

"I tell it pretty good."

"I'm sure you do, Mr. Spain, but since I can see the light at the end of the tunnel—"

"Hell, that's only an old carriage lamp."

"—I suspect we don't have much time."

Spain leaned over the steering wheel and squinted through the windshield. "Maybe, maybe not," he answered after a time. "But if I was you, I'd get somebody to tell me that legend before much longer. Sure would explain a lot of things."

Kent waited for the lightning, the earthquake, the flood, the fire, and finally sighed and said, "All right, Mr. Spain, keep me in no more suspense. Let's hear it."

"Sorry," the chauffeur said. "Too late."

And at the end of the foliage tunnel, where the trees were thickest, the mist heaviest, the light dimmest, and the carriage lamp hung from a rusted chain on a leafless tree, stood two fifteen-foot-high fieldstone pillars that marked the ends of a high stone wall smothering in writhing ivy. At eye level on each pillar was affixed a simple bronze plaque. On each plaque was engraved *Howe Manor* in stunning Gothic script.

"Just about there," Spain told him.

Kent began the process of bracing himself.

Once past the pillars, the contrast was astounding—another half-mile of gently curving tarmac drive, now flanked by luxurious island gardens, verdant croquet fields, several varieties of gazebos coyly thatched with bougainvillea, a diamond-shaped decorative pond in which a black-faced guard-swan apparently lived, and lined with trees tall and wide enough to fragment the sky.

And only when the trees fell away could he see the Manor itself.

Kent couldn't help it: "Mr. Spain, do you know anything about birthin' babies?"

"Sorry. Pretty good with a weed, though."

"Close enough."

It was three stories high, pure white, pure elegance, pure plantation. Doric pillars marked the deep red flagstone veranda which surrounded the house, holding up a balcony every upstairs room opened onto, including the hall Kent suspected ran front to back; gables poked out of the steep, slate, multi-angled roof; the windows were high and arched; chimneys proliferated and were used as nesting places by storks and sparrows and a raven that had ambition; and the front steps were four, wide, marble, and led to a pair of paneled oak doors massive enough to hold off the Union army.

To the right, a hundred well-tended yards away, a tall thorned hedge served as a diplomatic botanical screen behind which were eight small cottages, all white, all simple, all obviously handsomely redecorated slave quarters now used by those servants who were needed round the clock by the Howes and their guests; to the left a like distance were the stables that once held a full two dozen champion steeds, and were now home to four horses and a couple of fast cars, a station wagon, and a pickup that had the Howe crest on its doors.

As the car moved into the circular drive and headed for the porch, Spain pointed to the right. "My place is over there. Can't see the roses, though."

"I see."

"No kidding? Damn."

Kent opened his mouth, closed it, and rolled down the window. "Oh . . . lord."

"Swamp," Spain explained as the car hissed to a stop.

"I gathered."

He could smell it.

It smelled like dead things and rotting things and things that ought to be dead and rotting and weren't and didn't have the brains to know it. The fact that there were perhaps scores of roses and marigolds and honeysuckle vines and magnolia trees and ornamental orange and pear trees cleverly scattered around the property only served to create an amazing mixture of aromas that made treacle seem sour.

But at least, he thought as he climbed out of the car, it was cooler here. If he was lucky, his olfactory organs would shrivel within minutes, and then he wouldn't have all that much to complain about.

The doors opened.

A woman stepped out.

As Joe Bill lunged for the trunk, Kent smiled, and decided that perhaps things wouldn't be quite that bad after all, even if he hadn't heard about the mysterious Howe legend.

Della Depew sat in a booth in her bar and put the finishing touches on her weekly accounts. Once the ledger was closed, the pen stuck in her hair, she leaned back and sighed contentedly, looked around and sighed again.

She liked to describe her establishment as a little bit rustic, a little bit comfortable, and just a little bit this side of this-building-is-condemned. It contained unwashed, unpainted, untreated, bare-splinter walls, wobbly barstools whose faded red seats had somehow managed to pucker into a soft point, mooseheads and stuffed eels mounted on every wall, two pool tables and a shuffleboard table, and a sparse early afternoon clientele that appeared to be two steps away from a good dose of embalming. But the food was decent, the liquor drinkable, and it kept her in groceries, clothes, and a bank account that wouldn't let her starve since, because she was also the only qualified nurse in town, working in the clinic never brought her a dime. Many folks, the tourists especially, believed she was scrimping and saving in order to get enough money to leave the Landing and move to the big city, where her skills would be better appreciated.

They were wrong.

She liked the Landing. The weather sucked pond water in the summer, of course, but the people weren't half bad, she was a train ride away from a good time in the city, and she had her privacy out here. She wouldn't ever get rich, but she wouldn't get ulcers either.

Besides, if she weren't here, she wouldn't have seen that man riding in Joe Bill's car. It wasn't much of a look, but it had been enough to tell her that maybe she would accept Howe's invitation to tonight's party after all. It sure would beat hanging around here, waiting for the drunks to fall off their stools.

"How sad," a falsely deep voice said.

She looked up and saw a white balloon with a dark-tan face, thick salt-and-pepper hair brushed straight back from a brow multi-furrowed, and an unlit, unwrapped cigar shoved between teeth too white to be real.

"Stonewall," she said, "what the hell do you want?"

The mayor chuckled, waggled a *I just can't put anything over on you can I* finger at her, and sauntered as best he could up to the booth. "Scoot on over there, Della, that's a good girl." He shoehorned in beside her, using double-pump hip action to shift her when she made no attempt to provide room on her own. "Yep," he said, "real sad. You could be rich, y'know. Richer'n God."

She rolled her eyes and wondered what had prompted him, after a long and blessed week of silence, to trot his damn speech out again. He knew her answer, she knew her answer, and none of this would get them anything but heartburn.

He ignored the look, pulled the cigar from between his lips, and examined it. "Y'know, Della, holding onto a couple hundred acres of prime bottomland and then some, and giving up a fortune by not selling, that just don't make no sense, do it?" He sighed, and poked the cigar back into his mouth. "Sometimes I just don't understand the fair sex."

A semiconscious customer at the bar sneezed, straightened his pointed hat with all sorts of silly symbols on it, and demanded "a little attention here" before the sun went down and the prices went up. Della, seeing that the mayor wasn't about to do the gentlemanly thing, blithely climbed onto the table, walked to the edge, and jumped lightly to the floor.

Weathersly sputtered.

Della poured the customer a drink and suggested he leave before he started seeing monsters and little green men pissing in the corner.

"No call for that kind of talk," the mayor scolded.

The drunk drank, sneezed, gathered a huge book to his scrawny chest, told her that if she wanted a love potion or gator repellent just to call him, no charge, and left.

"Who the hell was that?" Stonewall demanded.

"Claims he's a wizard," she told him as she rinsed out the glass. "Comes in every day, scribbles in that book of his, gets drunk, leaves." She grinned. "Same old shit, Stoney, same old shit."

"Hey, watch your mouth!"

Della shrugged.

The mayor muttered something about the drunk not looking like a wizard; Della muttered something about the love potion not working either; the mayor sighed and wondered what kind of town this was, just anyone could come in, write a book like that idiot Roger Ace, and leave without putting him in it. Life just wasn't fun no more sometimes.

Della wiped down the bar. "You want something, Stonewall? A drink, I mean?"

Weathersly folded his arms on the booth table. "Now look, Della, we're both men of the world here, so to speak. Hell, I been to St. Louis, I know the score."

Four-to-one, she thought, and instantly covered her mouth and swallowed.

The mayor spread his arms. "I mean, can't you just see it, Della?" He pointed to the wall, as if it were a window on the world he described. "Just think of it—the Bayou Blast, complete with water slides, merry-go-rounds, picnic grounds, food tents, and a speedway. It's gonna be the best thing that ever happened to this place since we drove out the Union army." He pointed at her with the cigar. "And you could make millions with that land just rotting out there, home for nothing better than some lonely porcupines and old gators."

"I like old gators," she countered with a sweet smile.

Weathersly groaned. "Della, you're just getting yourself in one heap of trouble acting this way. All I'm trying to do is lend you a hand."

She held the smile.

The mayor began to flush, coughed into a fist, and looked at her sideways. "Big guns coming this way, y'know."

The smile wavered.

"Ol' Montague, he even brought in a baron."

She remembered the man in Joe Bill's car. "Baron?"

"Sure. Come here to check things out, probably representing some huge international conglomerate what's gonna make us all an offer we can't refuse."

"He's a baron?"

"He's a fruit," the mayor said, "in a blue suit, but he's still a baron guy. And if you know what's good for you, Della Depew, you'll—"

At which point a young woman slammed through the front door, dragging a little boy behind her.

"He saw it!" she cried to the bar. "My God, Timmy saw it!"

Silas grunted to his feet, scratched himself in several places at once, and said to Rude Humpquin, "I'm going. I think I blew it. I think that fella was the one."

The stationmaster shook his head sadly. "Silas, truth to tell, I don't think you'd know him if you saw him."

"Sure I would. Man had on a blue suit, weren't wearing a tie. Silliest thing I ever saw."

"Not that one, the other one."

"Oh." Silas kicked his wooden leg at a post. "Tell you the god's honest truth, Rude, I think you're right. Granddaddy never did explain exactly what I was Watching for. Wonder if he meant something else?"

"Could be."

Silas shrugged long-suffering resignation. His whole life devoted to something he didn't know about. How miserable. How pathetic. Good thing the pay was good; he'd feel like a damn fool otherwise.

"Say," Rude said then, cupping a hand around one ear. "Say, what's all the commotion down the street?"

Silas cupped an ear. Noise, for sure; it sounded like a lot of people shouting all at once about some damn thing or other. This far away, he couldn't make out the words. He checked the time—it was just shy of four. So it weren't that Blanche was sunbathing in the park again. Couldn't be that Sheriff Torn had caught him his first criminal. Some workers were leaving their jobs, but it was too early for the Friday riots when the farmhands came in from the fields. Which reminded him, as he and Rude walked to the parking lot, that he couldn't go home yet, even if he wanted to. There was still a hundred dollars cash money in his hip pocket he had to spend at Della Depew's, according to family tradition, after which Henry Fleuret would have to carry him home in the back of his truck.

Damn.

"Can't tell nothing," Rude said.

Silas squinted toward Main Street. "Can't see nothing."

The noise abated.

"Hang a minute," the stationmaster said, and hurried back to lock up his office. There weren't any trains due until Monday, and there was no reason for him to stick around, looking colorful. When he returned he offered to walk Silas to Depew's, maybe have a small libation before heading off for dinner.

Silas appreciated it.

Rude said it was nothing.

Silas said he still appreciated it, especially when he had this terrible feeling in his pegleg.

"Storm coming?" Rude asked.

"Yep," said Silas, "but not what you think."

"Are we going to die?" Jonelle Fleuret asked the cabin in general.

Jacques, standing at the door and peering through a small hole his mother had made with a flying frying pan formally aimed at Uncle Pier's skull, shook his head. "Don't be silly," he told her. "We just wait until Poppa comes home."

Something large, and probably quite unsightly, splashed angrily around the island.

Birds shrieked in fear.

Louisa cowered beside him. "I think we ought to make for the truck, get the hell out of here."

He looked at her, looked at his sister, looked at his uncle, who was sitting on the couch and whittling spears out of logs, and hated to admit that she was probably right. Staying here, if anything really was out there, wouldn't save them. That gator had been torn apart, not cut; that gator had been partially eaten, not ravaged by time and the tiny denizens of the swamp; that gator was a sign.

The splashing stopped.

Louisa looked at him, a hand on his arm.

He trembled.

She smiled and rubbed her cheek against his shoulder. "You going to marry me when this is all over and we can look back on it and laugh?"

His eyes widened. "We're cousins!"

Louisa Chuteaux winked. "Guess what?"

"What?"

"I've got a secret."

Something large, probably very unsightly, and definitely damn strong, slammed into the back wall.

Jonelle screamed.

Uncle Pier screamed.

Jacques swung the Remington around and hoped to hell it was loaded.

The woman who stood on the Manor porch was young, but not so young that her loose-fitting white shirt, snug white jeans, and tight white thigh-high boots didn't proclaim a certain physical maturity Kent had no difficulty admiring without being plebian about it. Her hair was long and dark and flowed about her shoulders, her face angular without being harsh, the black velvet choker about her neck a stark contrast to the milk tones of her flawless skin.

She wore, however, an unconscionable amount of makeup for this time of year, Kent decided, although it certainly didn't do her any harm, making her skin look so flawless and all.

"Your lordship," she said in a deeply sensuous voice, and held out a hand. "I am Arlaine Howe. We're so pleased you were able to join us."

Kent took a step up, brought the hand to his lips, and did the best he could not to nip off a knuckle when he heard the chauffeur drop his suitcase, and something of a glassy nature shattered inside. "Charmed," he said.

At that moment, another woman stepped out and stood beside the first. They could have been twins save the second had hair so blonde and eyebrows so thick and dark he couldn't be sure they were entirely real. Not that it was an unpleasant combination, to be sure and not that the two women together didn't somehow lend promise, if not a certain illicit excitement, to the impending affair this evening, but for some reason he began to feel as if he were faced by two very clever spiders. Black widows. Except for the blonde. It was a churlish sensation. He scolded himself for it. These, after all, were the daughters of his host. Even if one did use a bit too much eyeshadow.

"Bambi Howe," the second woman said, gracefully extending her hand.

He kissed it lightly. "Delighted, my dear."

Joe Bill choked and dropped the suitcase again.

On the other hand, their smiles made him feel uncomfortably like a child who had just passed a crucial but unknown test in deportment.

"Bambi," Arlaine said then, "please see that Joe Bill brings the baron's luggage to his room and makes things comfortable for him."

"Joe Bill," said Bambi, "please bring the baron's luggage to his room and make things comfortable for him."

The chauffeur saluted, hitched a suitcase under each arm, and managed to stumble up the steps and into the house without colliding with more than one pillar. He didn't look back with a single significant glance, which Kent found rather significant, and foreboding.

"Well," he said, scanning the manor grounds.

"My father," said Bambi, "is sorry that he is unable to greet you himself."

"There is a small problem," continued Arlaine, "which requires his immediate attention."

"He will, however," Bambi added, "endeavor to have a word with you before the guests arrive this evening."

"If he can," Arlaine emphasized.

"I thought I made that clear, Sister," Bambi said with a bright smile.

"Well, Sister," Arlaine responded with an even brighter smile that rippled her makeup, "the gentleman is, after all, not of our native shores and perhaps requires a certain modicum of clarification."

"Darling," Bambi said, hands clasped before her, "he speaks English."

"Yes, but—"

"Excuse me," Kent said.

They looked down at him.

He plucked apologetically at his heat-wrinkled jacket. "If we stand here much longer, ladies, it'll be night before you know it, and as you can see, I am not dressed for the occasion." He smiled. He gestured politely. He indicated with a slight nod known only to Scots barons who are royally pissed off, that perhaps they should get the hell out of his way so he could go inside and prepare himself for the party, or whatever the bloody hell was going on, because he sure didn't know and wasn't, to be honest, all that thrilled by his ignorance.

The Howe sisters translated, hesitated, finally parted, and as he passed between them, each took an arm.

Their perfume was subtle yet beguiling, their touch appropriately light yet tantalizing, their conversation as they passed over the threshold so airy and filled with Southern belle fluff that he instantly suspected they were hiding something. He didn't know how, and he didn't know why, and he didn't know what, and he definitely didn't want to know; but he knew with a soundless sigh that it was true. He had been in too many of these damn situations before—though, he admitted, never with twins—not to understand that something was not quite right in the paradise called Howe Manor.

And they still reminded him of spiders.

"Welcome to our humble home," the sisters proclaimed in unison once they were inside.

"Ah," he exclaimed approvingly.

The central hall was huge—fringed Oriental carpets, gold-framed family oil paintings on blue-and-white-and-gold walls, two teardrop chandeliers at least fifteen feet high suspended from brass chains, several Victorian wing chairs with tiny Sheraton tables between them, and a massive red-carpeted staircase that fanned upward to a gallery off of which he could see two hallways that evidently extended the width of the mansion in each direction. Closed double doors led to rooms right and left; the hall narrowed somewhat and vanished toward the rear.

The twins released him.

"Splendid," he said. "Quite worthy of a palace, don't you know."

The sisters preened without moving a muscle.

Kent groaned silently. You did it, he told himself; I can't believe you actually said *don't you know*. Jesus.

Then Bambi said, regretfully, "If you'll excuse me, m'lord, I must attend to the kitchen. The help is so unreliable these days, and I must be sure all is going smoothly."

"I understand perfectly," he replied, sketching a gallant bow as she moved away, wondering as she did how they decide how much flex to put in denim, because if she had been wearing a hoop skirt she would have cut half the population of Louisiana off at the knees.

At the same time, Arlaine stepped toward the doors on the left. "And I must leave you as well," she announced regretfully. "The staff is even now preparing our modest ballroom for this evening's modest entertainment, and I simply cannot trust them to set the chairs and music stands properly. I'm sure you understand."

"I certainly do," he agreed.

She opened the doors just enough for her to slip through before looking back and nodding toward the gallery. "Your room, sir, is the first one on the right. Mr. Spain will no doubt be waiting for you."

The doors closed.

No doubt, Kent thought; no doubt.

Don't you know.

Dear God in heaven, you're cracking up.

He inhaled slowly, shook his head, and wandered about the hall for a while, touching mediocre blind-eyed statues mounted on ornate marble pedestals, examining the oils from near and afar, once hunkering down to peer closely at a carpet. The bloody staff, he thought as he straightened and headed up the stairs two at a time, hasn't dusted or vacuumed this place in forty years, for Christ's sake.

More intrigue, Montana?

More suspicions?

Or is it just your imagination that eyeshadow-Arlaine and for-god's-sake-Bambi were measuring you not for a quick tumble in the plantation hay, as it were, but for a coffin? Were their eyes admiring your baronial aura, or trying to decide how much trouble you'll cause when they slip into your room tonight and cut off your head?

He grinned at the images he had conjured.

Old Southern manses did that to him.

So did paranoia.

What the hell? He was here, he wasn't going anywhere until Monday, what did he have to lose?

The answer, when it came, was so quickly suppressed that he couldn't even remember the question. It had to have been stupid, though; he was getting pretty good at querying the obvious.

"Joe Bill!" he called as he rounded the corner of the gallery and headed for the hallway that led to his room.

A muffled voice answered.

He looked down at the first floor, at the front doors, and held on to the polished walnut railing for a moment. Listening. Trying to hear the sounds of staff members being put smartly through their paces.

He heard nothing.

"Joe Bill!" he called again, turning.

And only barely suppressed a shriek when the pale-faced chauffeur, standing not two feet away, grabbed his arm and yanked him into the hall.

"Baron, you gotta see this, you ain't gonna believe it, I swear to god I nearly messed myself."

Kent was too astonished to protest the heavy-handed behavior, and too amazed when he was ushered into his room somewhat larger than an Omaha hotel, and saw, sitting on a Boston rocker by a window overlooking the back yard, a rather fat black woman dressed in calico, her head encased in a crimson turban, her feet shod in fluffy pink slippers.

When she saw him, she smiled.

He smiled back and whispered sideways to Spain, "So?"

"So?" Spain whispered sideways back. "She was here when I got here. Figured you knew her."

"Never saw her before in my life. Besides, I just got here, you great idiot."

"No call for that kind of whisper, Baron."

"I apologize. I'm under a strain."

"Right," the chauffeur said. "So who is she?"

Kent, sensing a prolonged conversational echo in the making, stepped forward. "Madam," he said, "you have the advantage."

Her smile did not waver.

"I am Kent Montana," he said.

"No, you ain't," she said. "You dead."

·2·

The turmoil within the bar continued for some time before Della had had enough and bellowed for order. The drunks immediately left for the next bar up the street, and the mayor blustered, but vacated his booth so that the frantic woman and the little boy could slide in. Della took the seat opposite and grabbed the woman's hands. "Bessy, calm down, calm yourself. You're just scaring the child."

The commotion outside, however, continued unabated.

"Breathe, Bessy, breathe," Della told her calmly.

Bessy Lou Leigh, her face flushed and gleaming with perspiration, her bosom heaving, her arms trembling and covered in goose flesh, closed her eyes and took several deep breaths. The boy simply looked around, wide-eyed, fascinated, and clearly not as frightened as his mother.

The mayor edged toward the door.

A minute passed. Another. Shouts, cries, and other exclamations of disbelief, fear, and cautious skepticism could be heard moving up and down the street. Della glanced up at the door, took a deep breath herself, and waited until Bessy Lou at last opened her eyes, smiled tremulously, and nodded that she was all right, she was in reasonable control and it would be nice if the nurse let the blood back into her hands.

Suddenly the boy declared earnestly, "I seen it, Miss Depew. I seen it. I seen the gopher!"

The mayor stopped edging.

Bessy Lou gasped and shook her head in dismay.

"I did," Timmy insisted.

Della smiled tolerantly, released his mother's hands, and leaned back with arms folded to give him her best *watch it kid I'm a nurse and I've heard it all so don't shit me* stare. She hoped that whatever story the tyke was about to tell wasn't going to ruin her chances of meeting a real baron. Not that she had any expectations, of course, but the more she thought about it, the more she realized that she had seen that face before. Somewhere. Which confused her, because it was—on the face of it— impossible. She'd never met a baron before, and certainly not one who rode in the back of Joe Bill's bloated Mercury. And she was positive she had never met that man before. So why the hell did he seem so familiar?

She blinked.

She looked at the boy, who was staring at her oddly. When she smiled, he cringed, and suddenly she realized what time it was. "Timmy, why weren't you in school today?"

Timmy Leigh looked confused at the unexpected change of subject. "Well, I . . . I . . ." He blushed and looked sideways at his mother before blurting, "I wanted to get the swamp treasure for my momma so she could be rich and marry Mr. Ace and we could buy a big house in Memphis and never have to come back here again."

Bessy Lou blushed worse than her son.

Weatherly jammed his cigar back between his lips and looked skyward for guidance.

Della asked the mayor to grab a cold can of soda pop from behind the bar and bring it over. "I see," she said to the boy. "And what was it you think you saw out there that made you come back without this great treasure of yours?"

Timmy looked around, suddenly fearful.

Her expression softened, and she reassured him that there was nothing to worry about, nothing to be afraid of; no one here was going to whomp or spank or otherwise shorten his life sooner than he expected. He was with friends, and he was safe. Besides, he was the star here.

"I am?"

She nodded solemnly. "And you saw something."

"I did."

"What did you see, Timmy, when you were supposed to be in school with your momma?"

"Sorry, momma," he said, turning to her.

"That's all right, Timmy," Bessy Lou told him, and gave him a fierce hug that nearly popped off his ears. She looked at Della, looked at the mayor. "He didn't actually see it, Della, to be honest. Not with his own two eyes. But he saw . . . lord help us, he says he saw the nest."

"Bull," the mayor snapped, slapping the pop can on the table and stomping away.

"Wait!" a voice cried from the doorway.

"Roger!" Bessy Lou cried in return, leaping up and opening her arms to embrace Roger Ace.

"I heard what happened," the young man said anxiously. He looked over her shoulder at Timmy. "Are you all right, son?"

"I seen it, Rog," the boy answered.

"So I heard." He looked at Della. "What do you think?"

Della told him she didn't know, since she hadn't heard the whole story yet, but it seemed to her that even if Timmy were exaggerating a little, something sure as hell had scared the freckles off his nose.

Roger examined the boy's face carefully.

Della prayed that the baron she thought she knew was single.

The mayor yelled, "Bull!" again. "The tad's just trying to get himself out of trouble, which he wouldn't be in if his momma didn't let him play hooky every ten minutes."

"I don't!" Bessy Lou snapped angrily.

"Ha!" the mayor countered.

But he was ignored as Timmy, spurred by trepidation and the natural ability of a canny child to hog the limelight, told the harrowing tale of his clandestine trip into the inhospitable bayou. Of finding the curious nest many months ago. Of returning every few weeks to see what the curious egg had done. Of returning today in hopes of dragging the curious egg back to his house and making them all rich. Of being chased for just hours and hours, maybe even days, by something huge and terrible and horrible and really ugly that wasn't an alligator, he'd been chased by them before and knew exactly what they sounded like, and this wasn't it.

"You have?" his mother said angrily.

The mayor returned and said, "Bosh! You just spooked yourself, boy. There isn't a monster living in that bayou, for the Lord's sake. You just spooked yourself, that's all. Gave yourself the nerves over some possum's shadow."

"I did not!" the boy insisted tearfully.

"Did too."

"Did not!"

Weatherly jabbed the cigar in the boy's face. "And you went and told half the damn town, isn't that right? You got all these good people all worked up, scared half to death, ready to shoot at shadows and alley cats just because you spooked yourself silly when you should've been out there at the school learning your books and stuff!"

Roger glared. "Stonewall, knock it off! You're scaring the boy."

Weatherly glared back. "Well, what the hell has he done, huh, big-shot writer what never even wrote about his own mayor? Scaring the whole town!" He shook. He quaked. He leaned heavily on the table and smiled at Timmy the way a jackal smiles at a rabbit. "Now look, son," he said, softening his voice, "we ain't gonna yell at you just because you played a little hooky. We've all done that now and then. It's a part of growing up. There ain't nothing all that all-fired terrible about it."

"But—"

"Hush, boy, while I'm talking to you. This is your mayor speaking, even if you didn't vote for me in the last election. See, what I'm saying is, son, you got caught, and we understand, and there's no need making up weird stories about what you did, because you're not going to be punished. It's okay. Nothing to fear. It's okay."

He straightened, grinned at everyone, returned the cigar smugly to its place.

Timmy bowed his head. "I'm sorry," he said.

"No sweat," the mayor said magnanimously.

"But I did see the nest."

"Oh, for Christ's sake!"

"And something did chase me just forever, Momma, Rog, I swear it! It chased me right—" Suddenly, Timmy spun around, scrambled to his knees, and looked toward the door. "Right to the tracks," he whispered, biting the inside of his cheek. "Oh lord, Momma, I think it's coming to town."

Pier Granlieu stood in the middle of the chaos in the shack, several sturdy spears clutched in his hands as he faced the back wall squarely. "You kids get ready," he ordered without turning around.

Something smashed the wall again and several pictures toppled from their hooks.

"Uncle Pier," Jacques said with more courage than he felt, "I'm not going to leave you here alone."

Grunts and snorts and slobbering outside.

"You gotta, son," his uncle replied flatly. "That thing's gonna be in here any second, you gotta be on your mark, no time for playing hero."

Jonelle wept noisily.

Louisa said, "Thing's too dumb to use the damn door, what're we worried about?"

Jacques felt sweat slicking across his palms, rushing down his cheeks, crawling down his spine. His stomach was trying to find room behind his heart, and a twitch behind his left knee made his left heel tap the floor. He was scared, and he hated himself for it. He also knew the man was right, that he had to protect his sister and cousin from whatever it was that pounded the wall again, this time snapping a plank and letting fierce sunlight slant into the dusty air. Yet he couldn't see himself running away, not if it meant leaving his uncle behind to fight whatever it was that seemed determined to knock the only home he had ever known off its pins.

Another board snapped under yet another assault.

Jonelle wailed.

Louisa slapped her.

Jonelle slapped her back.

Jacques brought the shotgun to his shoulder and said, "Uncle Pier, stand aside."

His uncle didn't move.

"Uncle Pier!"

"I hear you, boy," the man said. He readied his spears. "You got the keys?"

Jacques nodded.

"I said, you got the keys?"

Another plank shattered, and they could see something large and dark with maybe a hint of red outlined by the sun stalking around the porch, gathering itself for another charge.

"Yes," the boy answered.

Jonelle sobbed.

Louisa grabbed the doorknob.

"Jesus Christ," Pier exclaimed, "do you know what the hell that thing is?"

Then the back wall exploded inward in a hail of splinters and straightened nails, and the last thing Jacques heard as he vaulted the porch railing behind his sister and his cousin was his uncle, screaming Cajun war cries, screaming Anglo curses, screaming Biblical plagues.

And then, simply screaming.

Wally Torn, six feet of weight-lifting muscle and a jaw that would crack a walnut, adjusted his gunbelt, rubbed his bare chest with one hand, and looked thoughtfully out the picture window at the deserted park.

"Wonder what all that yelling was about?" he said in a voice that made angels swoon.

The telephone rang.

"Maybe," he thought aloud, "Silas started the weekend early, the dumb one-legged poop."

Behind him he could hear Blanche talking to someone, and he frowned until he remembered that the telephone had rung. He turned slowly, scratching idly at one bare leg. And saw her sultry face pale as she listened. Nuts, he thought. Never fails. Every weekend some beanhead causes trouble, I gotta go pop 'em in jail, and then clean up when they throw up. What the heck kind of a job is that for a man?

Blanche hung up.

Wally combed his thick silky hair with one hand. "Well, sugar, what's the trouble?"

"It's back," she said, dropping weakly into her chair.

"The train?"

"Zergopha."

He frowned. "What's that?"

She pointed a quivering finger at the papers strewn over the Persian carpet. "Didn't you read anything?"

"Oh." He frowned again. "That."

"I feel faint," she declared.

Wally ignored her. She was always feeling faint. She was always, for that matter, feeling some damn thing or other, which he actually didn't mind as long as it was him, but this was something else entirely. If what he had read was true, then he didn't remember half of what he read and would have to ask her to explain it to him again. Which he didn't mind all that much because Blanche explained things better than anyone he'd ever known, including the tourist from Austin who thought Wally looked a lot like Gary Cooper, who he didn't know but figured was someone pretty good, considering the way the tourist lady explained it to him.

He stared at the papers.

Zergopha.

He squinted.

Some kind of critter?

"Wally, darling," Blanche whispered.

Something to do with . . . the Manor?

Whatever it was—and it would come to him, give the man time, for crying out loud; he was under a lot of pressure these days what with the Blast and the party and crime and all—it was also going to make him rich as sin. That's what Blanche said, and she hadn't lied to him yet.

But what in swamp fever's name was it?

Darn, this job was a pain in the neck sometimes. It was hard enough sorting out the keys to the cells in the jail Mr. Howe had built for him nine years ago; how in the name of heck was he going to be able to sort out all the stuff that was in these papers, even if it was gonna make him rich enough to retire to New Orleans and own his own riverboat and buy Blanche more clothes than she knew what to do with, even if she hardly wore them anyway?

"Wally, honey?"

He stood, flexed a couple of muscles to keep himself in shape, and strode manfully to the desk. Blanche smiled. He smiled back and lifted the receiver of the sissy telephone she'd gotten the doc to buy her.

"Who you calling, sugarplum?"

"The Manor," he answered firmly. "Mr. Howe will know what to do."

"Oh my, how you talk," she said, fanning herself.

He cradled the receiver between neck and shoulder, and stared at the dial. Thought. Thought hard.

"You want me to do it for you, hound dog?"

He grinned. He loved it when she talked like that.

She punched the numbers.

He hitched up his gunbelt.

She said, "Wally, don't you think you ought to put on your pants?"

"Later," he said.

"Oh my oh my."

Then someone answered the phone at the other end, and he straightened, almost saluted, when he said, "Mr. Howe? Mr. Howe, this here's Sheriff Torn. I think I think I have something you ought to know about."

He listened.

He said, "The gopher."

"Zergopha," Blanche whispered huskily.

"Yeah, right, Zergopha."

While he listened he looked at the papers, looked at Blanche, looked back at the papers.

He hung up.

"Well?" she asked.

He hitched up his gunbelt. "He cusses a lot, don't he?"

"That's all he did?"

Wally frowned. "Yelled a lot, too."

She waited.

He blew out a breath, feeling like he was in school again, and he hated it. "He said I was to check around town, make sure nobody saw nothing, then call him back."

Blanche nodded. Stood. Walked around the desk and began to gather the papers together. "Wally," she said as she worked, "you do just that. And when you get back, we'll have something else to tell Mr. High-and-Mighty Howe." She held up Doc Pruit's extensive, damning notes. "Getting rich, remember?"

He smiled. "Of course I remember."

"Good." She pointed to the chandelier. "Then put your pants on and get moving. I'll explain it all to you later."

"Again?"

She grinned.

He grinned.

And sometimes, he thought, he didn't really hate this job at all.

"Custard!" Myrtle Mae yelled excitedly into her phone.

"Oh fiddle," said Gert. "We was just blowing out the candles, too."

·3·

The sitting room of Kent's bedroom suite contained a three-cushion couch, two brass-studded club chairs, a Boston rocker, several side tables, and a sideboard with a complement of filled decanters and stubby crystal glasses, all of it defined by a nine-by-twelve fringed Oriental carpet of such intricate floral design it reminded him of a peacock who didn't know which way to turn.

The fat woman remained in the rocker.

Joe Bill Spain, at Kent's request, sat on one of the armchairs.

And Kent sat on the couch, gazing through the open French doors to the balcony outside. A breeze fluttered the gauzy white curtains. The scent of magnolia and apricot wafted through the room. A small green lizard darted along the balcony's white railing. He watched until it tried to nail a Monarch butterfly with its tongue, missed, and fell off.

Could be an omen, he thought.

"I've something mighty important to tell you, Baron," the rotund woman known as Wandalina LeJermina said in a voice smooth as buttermilk on a warm summer day. "A story I declare I truly think you ought to hear."

"The legend," Spain said with a sharp nod.

The woman smiled at him.

"I could tell it if you want."

"No need, Joe Bill."

The chauffeur twisted his cap in his hands and pouted. "Nuts. I can tell it real good. You should hear me. Scare the warts off a dead frog the way I tell it, sound effects and everything."

The woman reached over and patted his hand. "I know that, Joe Bill, but we don't want to scare the warts off the baron, now do we?"

"Why not?" Spain answered. "Ain't gonna do no good otherwise. You don't put the fear of God into him, he ain't gonna believe you."

"Oh, I think he'll believe me."

"Oh," said Kent, "would you mind telling me what you two are talking about as if I weren't here?"

"Damnit, the legend," Joe Bill said. "I told you about that."

"Yes. I suppose you did."

"Damn right. Now she's gonna tell it and not scare the warts off you."

"For which," he replied, "I shall be eternally grateful."

"Well, now," said the woman, "I wouldn't be too sure about that."

And before Kent could stop her, she began.

Back there in the swamp, real deep in there, in a place previously known only to a lost tribe of five nameless Indians; a family of three Cajuns, all of whom had the same name; and an elderly moonshine tycoon that nobody in their right mind would have put claim to, much less a name—and all of whom were dead now anyway—a twisted and horrid and really disgusting shadow kind of thing splashed stolidly through the shallow water. Slowly. Purposefully. An unerring and uncanny sense of direction guided it through the darkest nights, the fiercest storms, the worse droughts, and the longest bouts of hunger only a step away from starvation.

It was large, but not terribly big.

It was ugly, but tolerably so.

And it had a brain which was, at the moment, teeming with unbidden racial memories, memories of a time when its mother and father had trod this same watery path many decades ago, before most of our times, killing and eating and slashing and slicing, and all the while attempting to exact ghastly revenge on their creator.

For so it was that they, these creatures of the swamp, were not naturally born. If indeed it could be said that they were born at all in the sense of which we are aware, theology aside for the time being. And they had come to learn this. And they had come to resent, despise, and otherwise not feel terribly benevolent toward not only this fact of their unnatural, and thus potentially blasphemous, life, but also toward the one they only knew as their creator.

They had lived for revenge.

They had died unfulfilled.

Their creator had lived.

Later on he had died, of course, but not when they did, because he had known they were dead and so didn't have to sit up nights anymore with a loaded shotgun in his lap and several sticks of touchy dynamite in his pockets, worrying about whether or not they were going to kill him. If he had known, however, what had happened before they died—what they had done and why— he probably would have killed himself and taken his chances elsewhere. Especially since he was the only one who truly knew exactly what they were, and why they were, and how they were going to react when they discovered he had cheated them.

He was right.

They were annoyed.

But they hadn't lived long enough to exact their vengeance.

At least not right away.

For, not long before their unnatural instincts warned them their unnatural time was nearing its end, they had retreated into that dark part of the swamp where the Cajuns and the Indians and the elderly moonshiner lived, and they had mated in a ritual as old as Time itself, a fairly loathsome act that lasted damn near five weeks and flattened a lot of trees and two of the Cajuns. When it was over, the ritual fulfilled, the male expired, as was the custom of the species, and the female used his corpse for a series of cannibalistic feasts designed to maintain her strength and strength of purpose. She hadn't minded. It was the way of things. It was her nature, as unnatural as it was. Regrets, of course, she had a few; but then again, too few to mention, since it was his flesh and bone that enabled her to sustain the life growing within her.

Possums were just too damn hard to catch in her condition.

Some years later, the result of that union was brought into the world.

Far away from the eyes of Man.

And since neither mother nor son—for indeed it was a son for those who got close enough to notice such things, were ever seen together, the remaining Cajun and a couple of the Indians assumed it was the same beast.

A mythical beast.

A fiend spawned by the swamp and fed by the full moon.

A creature that lived forever.

They gave it a name, a profane name, a demonic name, and that name became the name of the legend which surrounded it, which legend cropped up every year or so when animals disappeared and people disappeared and nothing at all was left behind except a long red feather that looked suspiciously like a scale.

Its name was Zergopha.

Its only translation is Death.

The Fleuret family pickup blew a front tire less than two miles from the island. After skidding the vehicle to a halt, Jacques pounded the steering wheel with a white-knuckled fist and cursed mightily, fluently, and in three healthy languages, much to the delighted yet apprehensive astonishment of his sister and cousin, and climbed out onto a rutted road not much wider than the truck itself. He didn't pay any attention to the sounds of the swamp; couldn't see more than two feet into the underbrush anyway, it was so thick. All he cared about was getting the *sacre bleu* flat fixed so he could get them all to the Landing before whatever it was that had killed his uncle picked up the trail and caught up with them.

"You need help?" Jonelle asked in a tiny, distressed voice as she leaned out the window.

"No," he said angrily. "I do not need help. I am perfectly capable of changing a tire by myself."

Her lips quivered.

He felt abruptly heartsick. "It's all right, Jonelle. I did not mean to snap at you. I'm just . . ." He flapped his arms helplessly.

Louisa leaned out the other window waving a spear she had rescued from the shack. "You going to hurry?"

Jacques glared at her.

She popped back into the cab.

Jonelle looked anxiously back the way they had come. "Jacques, what are we going to do?"

"Get out of here, silly," he said with a feigned laugh. "Just a minute or two and we'll be on our way."

It wasn't until he looked into the bed, and realized that he'd forgotten the spare again, that he also realized they weren't alone. He hurried back to the cab and told them they'd have to walk. Surprisingly, Jonelle didn't seem to mind. She was on the ground and moving before he could stop her, and Louisa, after what seemed to be perfunctory grousing, quickly followed, her spear cocked over her shoulder.

Shadows snapped across the rutted road.

The wind snapped through the high crowns of the trees.

Leaves too soon dead scuttled across the earth and huddled in trembling piles against protruding roots and rotting logs.

Jacques clutched the Remington close to his chest as he followed the women. He was scared, but he dared not show it. Not ten minutes after they abandoned the truck, he had heard a thrashing in the woods and had urged them into a slow trot. They dared not run, for running would exhaust them, and he knew instinctively that they would need as much reserve strength as they could muster when whatever it was that followed them finally broke into the open.

They moved silently.

Jonelle had grabbed a stout branch from the roadside and had snapped it expertly into a fair semblance of a staff; and dear Cousin Louisa was even now, at the trot, busily stripping a stout sapling she'd be able to use as a second spear.

Jacques's chest swelled with pride. Let the town children laugh at them for their country-swamp ways, let them call them names and try to trip them in the schoolyard, let them giggle at their worn but serviceable clothes—not one of those children could have prepared such an armory while simultaneously fleeing through the woods. Of course, if whatever followed them was as large as it sounded, if it was the same creature that had demolished their home—and there was no reason to believe that it wasn't—

that staff wouldn't be worth a hog's snout in a drought, and the spear wouldn't break a sweat. But it was, after all, the thought that counted.

Jonelle tripped and sprawled on her stomach with a terrified cry.

Jacques instantly yanked her to her feet.

Behind them the tearing, stomping, ripping, snorting, smashing, slapping, grunting sounds grew louder.

"Not far now," he panted. "Not far now." And wished his mother were here, preferably with one of her huge stew pots from the Manor.

A bird cried hoarsely overhead.

Something hissed at them from the growing darkness in the trees.

Louisa slowed until she matched Jacques stride for stride, her ponytail swinging side to side. "She's tired," she said, nodding toward Jonelle.

Jacques grunted his agreement.

"You gonna marry me when this is over?"

He looked at her in astonishment. Women, even when they were already sixteen, never ceased to amaze him. "But I told you—we're cousins!"

She shrugged. "My folks are dead, Uncle Pier never cared one way or the other, and we're not that close cousins." Then she winked. "Besides, I know something you don't."

She had already said that, but he hadn't doubted it the first time. She was the third smartest kid in the school; he wasn't sure he even had a number.

"A family secret," she teased.

He ignored her. It was panic talking. He saw it all the time in the movies. Death came floating and humming too close and folks started babbling all kinds of private things that everyone in the audience already knew anyway but the people on the screen were too busy saying their lines to figure it out. Louisa Chuteaux was simply trying to prove that she was as brave as he was, that's all it was. And he admired her for it. It was stupid, considering the circumstances, but he admired her nonetheless.

A slobbering, slithering, truly disgusting noise made him glance nervously over his shoulder.

He saw nothing.

Louisa, however, had sped up a little.

"Soon," Jonelle gasped. "Soon."

Not soon enough, Sis, Jacques thought when he looked back again and saw, far behind them, something stumble into the road. He could make out no details, could see little more than an outline, but he knew it wasn't a gator that had learned to walk on its hind legs.

He gripped the shotgun more tightly.

Louisa practiced with her staff.

He cast a sketchy map in his mind and realized they would never be able to make the Landing in time. "Hey!" he called. "Look, we'll have to take the fork, go straight to the clinic."

Jonelle huffed in puzzlement.

"The town is too far away. We'll . . . we'll never make it."

Louisa looked back at him with undeniable pride and teen lust in her smoldering green eyes.

What the hell, Jacques thought; what are cousins for, anyway?

Then the thing in the road roared.

Jacques stopped.

The others trotted on several yards before Louisa realized what had happened and called to her cousin. Quickly they hurried back and stared down the road.

Jonelle held her staff at the ready and demanded to know what in hell her brother was thinking of, stopping dead like that in the middle of a life-threatening flight.

"It's gone," Jacques said, his voice low and uneasy.

They peered through the dim light.

"He took off," the boy continued. And pointed. "Went that way."

"Oh damn," said Louisa. "He's heading—"

"Yes," he said.

Jonelle chewed her lower lip nervously.

"Well, hell, hot damn, what're we worried about?" Louisa said cheerfully. "He's gone, we don't have to run anymore."

Jacques shook his head. She was right in one sense, but in a larger, moralistic sense, their race had just begun.

"You can't mean it," his cousin said when she saw his expression. "What have they ever done for us? Everyone up there, they treat us like dirt. Scum. They don't even pay Aunt Matilda minimum wage."

"I don't care," Jacques said. "Zergopha is heading right for the Manor, and if we don't warn them, they're all going to die. My mother included."

"The gopher?" Louisa said.

He looked at her.

She shrugged.

Jacques was stung by her ignorance, but said nothing. They wouldn't be able to reach the Manor before Zergopha, which never in his wildest dreams did he really believe existed until he actually saw it and then still had doubts, but they could reach the clinic and borrow the car. The path the creature had taken wouldn't get it to the Manor's grounds until well after sundown, probably not until midnight, unless it knew how to fly. All that water, all that quicksand, all those bugs flying around and getting into its beady eyes—plenty of time to get to town and mount the rescue party. No sweat. But they had to move now, or they'd be too late.

To be stuck in the bayou, at night, would mean their deaths.

He started to walk.

"You can go with me or stay here," he said without looking around. "All I know is, I gotta do what's right."

"Damn," said Jonelle.

Louisa shook her head and, unwillingly, followed. "Hell," she said to the darkening swamp, "don't you just hate it when he talks like that?"

"Have you understood a single word I've said, Baron?" the roly-poly woman asked with a trace of impatience.

He looked at her and smiled. "Indeed I have, Miss LeJermina, indeed I have."

"And?"

He looked to Spain, who jumped to his feet. "Gotta go," the chauffeur said, slapping on his cap, rubbing his hands briskly. "Got other folks to pick up. In town. The mayor. People like that."

"Sit," Kent commanded softly.

Spain sat.

Kent contemplated the view again while he considered the utterly ridiculous, yet curiously compelling story Wandalina LeJermina had just told him. The legend itself, which most certainly did not scare the warts off him, didn't bother him all that much, because it was, of course, only a legend; the rest of it, however—the part that came after the legend that not even Joe Bill knew about, the part that had kept him from unpacking— had to do with Montague Howe's father's experimental experiments with the rather extraordinary biological and physiological similarities of humans in the form of white and black slaves—and a rare species of double-jaw-jointed alligator found only within a fifty-mile radius of this very plantation. The elder Howe, it appeared, had become fanatically convinced through his extensive studies of arcane scientific tomes that human beings who laid eggs, as alligators did, would be much more powerful and efficient than humans who had their offspring the old-fashioned way. To succeed would mean an inexpensive, inexhaustible, and guaranteed semiannual replenishment of a low-cost labor supply much too dumb to even think about forming a union. Food was no problem; they ate each other. To fail simply meant buying up another batch of slaves and trying again.

And since the legal practice of slavery had been abolished a century before, the purchasing of viable victims by the thrifty elder Howe for said experiments was done during holiday sales of the black market. Kidnap victims, runaways, the wandering homeless, and former politicians and movie stars of the "whatever happened to" variety.

That bit bothered him a lot.

He took a deep breath and exhaled slowly.

He sipped from what was left of the Glenbannock Spain hadn't lost by dropping the suitcase.

He looked at LeJermina and asked, "What does all this have to do with me? Why did you come to me and not go to the local authorities?"

"I'm not sure," she answered.

"You're not sure?"

She shook her head and nearly lost her turban. "Baron, I'm just a poor black woman who tries to make things right in a world where injustice and bigotry and secret laboratories run too rampant for my ordinary tastes." She swept a massive arm laden with gold bracelets toward the balcony, and her voice deepened impressively. "Like those brave souls who have gone before me, I still cling to the sacred and intrinsic belief that all men are created equal, that they have a right to a decent job at a decent wage, that evil in all guises must be uprooted and destroyed wherever discovered, that—"

"Never mind," he said wearily.

"Sir?"

"Now look, Baron," Joe Bill began.

Kent silenced them both with a look.

Damnit, he knew this woman.

He hadn't recognized her at first, but now he was positive he knew her.

Well, not this particular woman particularly, whom he had never seen before in his life and would have remembered if he had because that rocker wasn't ever going to be the same again once she stood up; but he most assuredly had met her type before. Dozens of times. Too many bloody times. In *Passions and Power* they showed up every couple of months, usually as a long-lost and generally short-lived, hitherto unknown family member or former neighbor who lets the cat out of the bag, puts the rooster in the henhouse, the fly in the ointment, and the grease on the wheel that keeps the plot and the ratings moving for another two or three months. Shortly afterward, they vanish, never to be seen again. As a butler, he had little to do but announce them to the lady of the house and so didn't much give a flying buttress; as an actor, however, he despised and detested them because despite their brief sojourns, they always had more, and more important, lines than he did. They also got a lot more mail.

"I just wanted to warn you," the woman said humbly.

Of course you did, he thought in a severe bout of resignation.

"You must understand that I could not in good conscience let Montague Howe carry on his father's work without somebody knowing what was going on."

Of course not, he thought as resignation was laced with a touch of depression.

Using the rocker as a slingshot, then, Wandalina LeJermina barreled to her feet, adjusted the folds of her skirts, and set her turban straight. "I must leave you now," she announced regretfully.

Sure you do, he thought.

She waggled a finger at him. "Y'all just take care now, y'hear? Y'all don't do something powerful stupid."

Bet on it, he agreed.

She smiled.

His own smile was painful.

She rolled out of the room and closed the door silently behind her.

He watched the door in case she should return, shook his head, and remembered something else he hated about her kind—they always had stupid names.

"Damn woman," he muttered at last.

"What woman?" Spain asked dully, shaking his head and rubbing his face as if he had just been released from a trance.

Kent pointed at him accusingly. "Joe Bill, damnit, you didn't tell me about the reputedly hideous experiments old Howe performed."

Spain blanched. "How'd you know about that?"

"We Scots know these things. We're fey."

"No shit," Spain said. He slapped his leg. "Damn, you don't look—"

Kent's glare put a cork in him; his hand directed the unavoidable unpacking of his belongings; his canny grasp of the situation broke the tumbler still in his hand, and he swore a lot while he looked for something to wrap around the cut; his stride and his eventually handkerchief-bandaged hand, took him out to the balcony where he looked down at the artful display of plant and tree in the yard below, at the tables and the colorful umbrellas that protected them, at the way the two sisters worked like demons to string Chinese lanterns among the branches, at the walk at the back where, unless he was seriously mistaken, there would probably be a hidden exit, beyond which would be something he had no intention of locating because, as soon as this sham of a party was over, he was hiking back to town where he would beg, borrow, or steal some mode of transportation and make his way back to his agent, who, if the man was lucky, might live.

He imagined the conversation:

Movie, my ass, you plaid-jacket freak. He's up to something and it isn't top billing. Monsters in a swamp, secret rooms, Conan the Chauffeur, my . . . god!

Kent. Baby. Don't count your chickens.
Agent. Jerk. Don't count your commission.

But if it wasn't a movie, why then was he here? Why him and not some other poor slob of an unemployed actor? Of course, he wasn't a poor slob, or even a slob by many civilized standards, but he was definitely unemployed, and damn tactless it was of everyone to keep reminding him of it. But why him? What was there about him, and no other, that had caused Montague Howe to seek him out among the billions of souls who lived on this planet? What special—nay, unique—qualities did he embody that would drive a man like Howe to spend untold thousands just to lure him here? What—

"You finished?" Spain asked at his shoulder.

Kent looked at him.

The chauffeur shrugged.

Kent shook his head ruefully, laughed ruefully, sighed without an adverb in sight, and said, "You know, Mr. Spain, I quite nearly laughed while that woman told her fantastic tale. In fact, I must admit I thought she said 'gopher' at the end there." He chuckled.

Spain leaned against the railing. "Baron, I don't know about over there in Scotland, but here in the good ol' U.S.A. there ain't no gopher that big in the whole damn world." He spat over the side. "'Course, being a practical man, I don't believe a word of it myself. I mean, something like that actually lived around here, a man would know it, wouldn't he? I mean, things like that, they just don't come knocking on your door asking to rampage your house, kill your family, run off with your children, stuff like that. They sneak around a lot, you know? Do spooky stuff in the swamp, make everybody jumpy, knock off a few folks what nobody cares about. I mean, stuff like that, a man would know it, right?"

Kent stared at him.

The sisters giggled as they tested the lanterns and scared the plumes off two peacocks.

A mournful cry in the swamp.

The lizard climbed back to the railing and blinked its large brown eyes.

Kent pointed dramatically at the reptile. "Notice, if you will, Joe Bill, what we have here before us—a distant yet obvious relative of those amphibious beasts who live out there in the bayou. Look closely at it, please. Examine it. Notice that it bears no conceivable resemblance at all to either one of us, even on our worst mornings. Notice that it eats, for god's sake, bugs and worms. So how the hell can anyone expect to splice a gene from here to there and there to here and expect to get something out of it?"

Spain examined the lizard.

The lizard fell off the railing.

"Actually," the man said, "it kinda looks like Silas."

Kent gave him the point and looked down at the yard, now ready for the soiree.

The twins looked up and waved gaily.

Spiders, he thought glumly.

And then, seemingly out of nowhere, a man appeared. A tall man. In white. Slightly stooped. With a white riding crop in one hand. A huge ugly dog at his side. The twins ran to him, scratched the huge ugly dog behind its ears, and hugged the man in a decidedly nonerotic manner.

"Oh shit," Spain whispered and ducked hastily back into the room.

Kent needed no such expletive.

He knew who the man was.

The man looked up from beneath the floppy brim of his white hat, and nodded.

Kent nodded.

The dog slobbered.

The twins waved.

The bedroom door slammed to mark the chauffeur's exit.

Nuts, Kent thought; dinner is served.

◆ 4 ◆

Montague Howe, arms still around his daughters, watched as the tall man left the balcony and retreated into his room.

"Is that him?"

Arlaine grunted.

"Yes, Daddy," Bambi said, squirming with excitement. "Isn't he just perfect?"

"You're sure that's the one?"

"No doubt about it."

"Ah."

Arlaine excused herself then and hurried into the house, her stride that of one who suffers much pain. Thor trotted after her.

Howe's expression darkened, his eyes narrowed. "Has she said anything?"

Bambi shook her head. "But I think it won't be all that long now, Daddy. She has some powerful aches now and again. I just don't . . . I just don't know how she stands it." She burst into tears.

Howe hugged her tightly, and released her.

"Daddy?"

"It's all right, child, it's all right. He is the man, and I am more than man enough for him." His smile fried a peacock. "As

89

long as I am alive, as long as there is always a tomorrow, I swear
to you that Arlaine shall never go hungry again!"

"Oh . . . Daddy!"

Howe breathed deeply several times, swallowed his emotions
which were too damn emotional for a man of his position, standing
out in the middle of the lawn like that where just anyone could see
him, and headed for the house.

"You be sure that man is here when it's time, Peaches," he
said over his shoulder. "You be sure."

"Oh, I will, Daddy," Bambi promised. "I will."

I know you will, he thought as he entered the house; because
if you don't, child, I'm going feed you to the dog.

·5·

Doc Pruit had heard the shouts on the street from his traditional place in the barber chair. Since the door was open, he had also heard a few choice words, none of which he liked, all of which had confirmed his earlier suspicion that Howe's Landing was on the downside slip straight into another Hell. Then the fat-headed mayor had come from somewhere, and within minutes the ruckus had died down to a tense but uneventful silence.

"A little off the sides, Mort," he said to the barber.

Mort Trusoe grunted. He never talked except in his sleep, and Doc and the others had long ago learned to read his noises instead.

"I wouldn't worry about it," Doc answered, fingers crossed under the sheet that covered him neck to knee. "Another one of them Bayou Blast rallies, I bet."

Mort sighed and whistled between his teeth.

Doc didn't mind being called a liar, especially when there was a pair of scissors expertly poised above his right ear; what he resented, however, was the way Mort had seen clear through him. He knew instantly the doc was worried, and although the barber wasn't old enough to have been alive when the first Hell came to Howe's Landing, he had heard the stories, just like all the others. And, like all the others, he neither believed nor disbelieved.

Anyone who had lived on the fringe of the bayou for any length of time knew that those shadowy waters hadn't ever been fully explored. Not by the white men, not by the Cajuns, not by the Indians. A couple of tourists, maybe, but they never came back. Which meant that there were *things* in there no one had ever seen, *places* that had never seen the full light of the sun.

So, Mort sighed and whistled on, who was to say that it couldn't happen again?

"No one," Doc admitted reluctantly. "You got some tint for that gray there? It looks like a faded rug. Don't want the folks at the Manor believing I'm getting old before my time."

Mort hummed.

"Very funny."

Doc watched his wall-mirror reflection floating above the witch hazel and comb disinfectant. He remembered the chill he'd felt earlier. He remembered how it had been so many years ago.

"Mort, you think I'm crazy, going up there tonight, knowing the only reason I was asked was so that the Howes could try to convince me to back the Blast and give my patients discounts if they did too?"

Mort stropped the razor slowly.

"Yeah, I think so too." He leaned back and let the hot towel settle over his face. Yet he was going. Why? Because he knew that what he knew somehow felt wrong. Howe didn't have to throw a party just to get all his enemies together; hell, he could do that just by walking down Main Street.

So what was he up to?

And why was good old Doc so smart that he was dumb enough to walk right into the lion's den?

Mort, as if reading his mind, chirped the song of a hunting hawk.

Right, Doc thought; what else was there to do on Friday night around here?

Stonewall Weathersly slumped wearily in his mayoral chair, braced the soles of his saddle oxfords against the windowsill, and looked out at the main street. His face was still red, sweat still stained his shirt, and his throat was still sore, but he was pleased with the way he had handled all them nervous nellies, sending them back to their homes feeling a lot better about

themselves and the man they had unanimously elected to this
office except for the fools that voted for Della Depew and damn
near caused a run-off. And except for Myrtle Mae, who had
practically sliced his suspenders with that damn knife of hers.
Accused him of lying right there in the middle of the street, of
all things! Hadn't been for Gert falling outta her walker because
the Thompson was so heavy, the old bag might've had snipers
on the rooftops by now, for lord's sake.

He snorted.

He chuckled.

He cut off a guffaw and mopped his face with a handkerchief.
No laughing matter, boy, he told himself, no laughing matter. If
he had taken up the standard against a mythical monster, and the
myth was exposed as it surely would have been, who the hell but
Republicans believed in monsters anymore?, he'd have looked
like a blamed idiot, and those pea-brains sitting on the Bayou
Blast fence would've come down solid on the side of that pain
in the ass Depew.

No telling what Montague would have said.

He wiped his face again.

Actually, he knew damn well what his partner would have
said, only his partner would have said it through that damn ugly
dog of his, and Stonewall Weathersly would now be nothing
more than a disgusting mess of his old self.

Lord, he thought, the things I have to do to keep things moving.
He suggested to himself that, after telling Howe of his heroics, he
hint about a larger cut in the proceedings. He considered it. It
sounded good. Better, however, he do it over the phone in case
he had to catch the train quicker than he'd planned.

A check of his watch told him he had less than two hours
before the Manor car came by to take him to the party. Which
reminded him of that baron fella. What in swamp gas perfume
was Montague up to? He scowled. He scratched the folds of his
neck. He recalled a TV show where some big-money guy in Las
Vegas hired this rich guy to kill another rich guy because nobody
would suspect a rich guy of being a killer. Especially when they
didn't know that the first rich guy got rich killing other rich guys
in the first place.

His right eye narrowed.

His left eye widened.

Made sense once you thought about it. You want to keep all the loot to yourself, you make sure there ain't nobody to share it with. Bring in a fruit in a blue suit, call him some stupid name like a baron, bring Weatherly out to the Manor with a bunch of other members of the Landing elite, take him into the swamp, and he'd never be heard of again. Terrible about the mayor, isn't it? Got drunk, wandered off, kept the gators burping right through Labor Day.

Son . . . of . . . a . . . bitch.

He didn't turn around when someone walked into his office without even Thury making an announcement.

"Mr. Mayor?"

"You got it first time outta the crib," he said, waving a lazy hand toward a chair.

The chair was pulled over to the window.

Something heavy was dropped on the desk.

"That what I think it is?" the mayor asked with feigned indifference and monumental control.

"Every last word of it."

"You think there's a suspicion?"

"Not a whit."

"You think ol' Montague got the wind up?"

The chair scraped closer. But not too close. "He knows about the tad and the gopher."

"Zergopha."

"Yeah, that too."

The major watched Doc Pruit leave the barbershop, sniff the air, and head for Della Depew's. Weatherly grunted in admiration. Stupid old fart fell for the speech hook, line, and yank the sucker home. No trouble from that quarter, he'd bet on it. He glanced at his watch again. "Gotta get ready soon for the do."

"Me too."

A penciled eyebrow lifted. "You going?"

"Of course. After all, I am a leading citizen."

The voice chuckled.

The mayor chuckled.

Thury screamed that someone had better hurry up and take his shower or that someone was gonna empty the Manor faster than spit blinds a possum.

The chair scraped hastily back to its original position. "Guess I'll just head along home. The back way, if that's all right with you."

The mayor waved languidly. "See you tonight."

"Not if I see you first."

The voice chuckled.

The mayor chuckled.

And as soon as the back door closed, he rubbed his hands delightedly and gave himself a silent cheer. Lordy, he did love a good blackmail and early retirement scheme. Especially one that had more double-crosses than two bishops and a zealous actress. And this one was gonna get him outta this godforsaken town faster than a gnat's blink. No way he can lose now.

No way at all.

He folded his hands across his belly, dropped his feet lightly to the floor, and swiveled around, eyed the package sitting so prettily on the blotter, then scooped it into a top drawer. Time to read it later. He already had an idea of what it said. And if it said what he already had an idea what it said, it was damn near as good as wearing bulletproof armor. The fruit in the suit was a good as disarmed.

He grinned.

He felt himself growing excited at the confrontation, the intrigue, the sparring, the dancing, the eating, the drinking he was gonna do tonight.

He panted.

He fanned himself.

He yelled, "Thury, get your pins in here, we got some dictating to do!"

"Thank God!" Thury hollered back. "I thought you didn't love me anymore!"

Bessy Lou Leigh's ancestral home was a modest single-story cottage located only a few yards off the main street, on Columbine Lane. Ivy-covered, with a white picket fence, roses in profusion in both front and back yards, and a chirpy parakeet in a gilded cage in the living room.

Roger sat on the floral-upholstered sofa and waited while, in the white-and-gold kitchen, Bessy Lou, in her own teacherlike fashion, blasted the hell out of her tearful son for playing hooky, going into the swamp without her permission, and telling tall tales that scared the town and his mother half to death and back. It was a formidable sound. It made the parakeet reach for the cord that hauled up its floral cage cover. It made Roger wonder what it would be like being married to that woman, whom he adored and worshipped and wanted to see naked as soon as possible, or at least before he was too old to enjoy it.

It also made him think about Zergopha.

Until now, and he hated to admit it but he was a writer and knew all about Truth and Other Stuff, his books had been mere supermarket throwaways, airplane seat-pocket stuffers, ridiculous plots and silly excursions into the spatial and temporal unknown and relationships with characters of which he had, thus far, no firsthand knowledge. True, they had brought him enough money to lure his dreams closer to reality than he'd ever dreamed; true, they sold well enough to provide sufficient fodder for his ego, which had damn near starved in the five-and-dime; true, they made Bessy Lou look upon him with, if not admiration, then a certain kind of respect.

But this was different.

This Zergopha business, if it was true, would make him millions. *If* he could only get it down fast enough and to the publishers quickly enough and onto the streets rapidly enough to beat the competition. Of which, as far as he knew, there was none.

He smiled.

He stood when Bessy Lou came into the room, flushed, a strand of her hair matted wetly to her brow, her bosom heaving and her hands twitching from her exertion. Of Timmy, he could hear nothing.

"I have an idea," he said before she could speak.

"Oh, Roger."

Impulsively he grabbed her hands and guided her to the couch, sitting so close he could feel the throbbing heat of her dissipating anger. He panted a little himself. "No, listen, Bessy, I swear this is going to be the best thing that ever happened to us."

He stopped.

She smiled coyly. "Us?"

"Well . . . in a manner of speaking, yes."

Her eyelashes batted; his forelock fluttered. "Roger Ace, are you taking advantage of my weakened psychological state by proposing marriage to me?"

"Well," he said.

She looked away, toward the ivy-rimmed window. "Roger, I surely do not know what to say."

"Then don't say anything," he told her, before she got the right idea at the wrong time. "Just listen for a minute." He proceeded to explain his nebulous idea of fortune-making as it related to Zergopha and its possible existence. When she protested that Timmy had, after all, a child's perfectly normal active imagination, even the mayor said so and Della didn't seem terribly convinced either, he responded by saying, "Then I'll just have to get a boat and go into the swamp and find that egg. If it's there, Timmy is telling the truth. If it's not, I'll marry you anyway."

Her eyes widened.

He swallowed his impetuousness with more than a little difficulty.

"You will go into that deadly swamp just to prove my little boy isn't a liar, a crier of wolf?"

"Did I say that?"

"You'll risk your life for me just to prove that you love me and my son above all else?"

He closed one eye, and not being one who made decisions in less than a couple of chapters, thought about it.

Bessy Lou gripped his arms. "You would dare snake venom, panther claws, gator jaws, and the possibility of coming face to face with the legendary Zergopha just to redeem my family's image in this gossip-mongering community?"

"Well, I'm not so sure I said the part about the jaws," he answered weakly.

But it was no use. She was too close. Her breath was too hot. Her skin was too warm. Her grip was too strong. He could either agree or learn to type with his toes.

"Hey, Momma, are you gonna kiss him or what?" Timmy asked mischievously from the doorway.

She did.

Roger gasped.

She did it again when Timmy applauded and volunteered to clean the rifle in the hall closet.

Roger checked his watch as best he could, what with his vision being doubled and tripled like it was. "It's getting late," he said.

"It's not that far," said Timmy eagerly. "If you borrow Silas Bouquette's skiff, it's got a motor on it, we could be out there and back in an hour. Long before dark, Mr. Ace."

Bessy Lou embraced him.

Her lips were scorching upon his ear.

"Millions," she whispered.

He looked at Timmy, glowing and grinning.

"Freedom," she husked.

He looked through the ivy-covered window and saw a shimmering Rolls Royce parked at the curb, with his initials engraved in silver on the door.

"Me," she hinted.

"I'll need my boots," he said.

Timmy yelled, "Hooray!" and ran for the closet.

Bessy Lou disengaged herself, fussed over the state of her clothes and hair, and said that she'd be right back, she was only going to change into something more suitable to crawling through the bayou.

Which left him alone in the room, wondering if he hadn't written too many adventures, seen too many futures, lived too many alternate lives to know what the hell he was doing.

The answer was No.

He had responsibilities now—to his readers and his new family. If ever there was a time to be a man, this was it. If ever there was a time to forge the metal of his soul, this was it. If ever he had hopes of the South rising again, this was them. There was no turning back.

Roger Ace was on the move.

Myrtle Mae Beauregard stood on her porch, honing her bowie knife on the portable whetstone hanging from the chain around her neck. Oh, she had heard the blather Stonewall had shouted in the street, defusing the excitement, making half the town laugh at her and Gert while the other half ran like hell for home to get ready for the party; oh, yes indeed, she had heard the scorn heaped upon little Timmy Leigh and the alleged falsehoods he told right there in the bar in front of his mother; and she had listened carefully to the mayor as he had stumped up and down the road, shaking hands, kissing babies, telling jokes, swatting fannies, pinching bottoms.

She had heard it all and didn't believe a word of it.

Nope, not on a bet.

When the mayor started acting like a politician, Myrtle Mae knew the bastard was lying through his teeth.

The others had been alerted. They had declared themselves ready. Even now she could hear Ethel June's bugle warming up.

She sighed her contentment.

She adjusted her camouflage hairnet.

Let them dance and drink and fornicate until dawn out there on the plantation, leaving the town she loved defenseless and without hope.

Myrtle Mae Beauregard was on the job.

~ III ~

Zergopha's Plan

Deep in the swamp, confused by the flying bugs and the clutching quicksand and the treacherous currents that made traveling pure Hell, Zergopha, newly hatched and thinking only of unadulterated, untainted, unsullied revenge, ate a porcupine for lunch and pretended it was the man who had given him life.

It was in no hurry.

Familial memory told it there was only one person alive who knew how to kill it, and that person was most definitely not the man who lived in the big white house at the edge of the bayou. Who that man was, exactly—the one who might destroy it—it did not know. And, frankly, it didn't care.

Zergopha knew it was invincible.

Zergopha knew that the man who had given it life knew that it was invincible.

Zergopha suspected that the only man in the world who could kill it didn't even know he could and therefore couldn't kill it, which is where the invincible part came in.

Therefore, it plucked another porcupine clean, swatted the hell out of those flying bugs that kept trying to lay eggs in the gaps between its scales, bounded over the quicksand without any trouble at all, and avoided the treacherous deep currents by staying away from them.

It slobbered, splashed onward, tore the head off an alligator and ate the brains for a snack, and finally, as the day's heat wilted the fluffy red feathers that sprouted where the scales didn't, it curled up beneath the comforting knees of a gnarled cypress tree.

Nossir.

Zergopha, invincible and cunning, was in no hurry at all.

– IV –

Howe's Plan

· 1 ·

Kent Montana stood before the full-length mirror affixed to the back of his bedroom door, adjusted the fall of his white suit jacket, brushed his lapels with the backs of his fingers, smoothed the front of his white shirt, adjusted the open collar, briskly wiped a hand over that portion of his white trousers he could reach without bending over, centered his belt buckle, used his palms to squash errant hairs back into place, adjusted the jacket again, flicked something unsightly off an elbow, adjusted the collar and lapels again, polished his shoes on his trouser legs, stepped back and concluded that nothing he could do would alter the fact that he looked like a goddamn ghost, or a confused angel wondering if it had been worth all the trouble.

A delicately, one might even say prissily, handwritten note on the dressing table, delivered while he had been taking a cool shower in the adjoining bathroom, had informed him that the dress for the evening's activities would be "casual"; a footnote explained that tuxedos, given the climate, were out of the question in an unairconditioned house; a scribble on the back suggested that jeans, chinos, and Bermuda shorts, of course, weren't casual, they were insulting.

Which left him with the white suit.

He sighed.

He returned to the sitting room, walked out onto the balcony, took a deep breath of mint-scented air, and watched as the sun began to tear itself apart in the tops of the bayou trees. Shadows freckled the grass. One set of birds was replaced by another, calling in the distance, echoing, falling silent, calling again. A breeze played around his hair and brought the temperature down to almost tolerable levels. He glanced at his watch, rubbed his wrist thoughtfully with a thumb, and decided to do a little exploring. After all, the Howes couldn't expect him to stay in his room the entire time. Like a prisoner. Like a bathing beauty in a birthday cake. Like a jack in a box. Like a prisoner.

Enough of that, lad, he told himself, and watched his friend the lizard stalk either a very dead or very slow ant on the railing.

What he had to do now was come to a quick but concrete decision, something he was reasonably good at when said decision involved things like forbidden experiments, critters out of legend, and the ultimate preservation of his aristocratic flesh and bone. The obvious thing would be to pack up and leave. Now. Assuming he believed LeJermina in the first place. The less obvious thing would be to stick around, mingle with the guests, whose automobiles he could even now hear guttering and roaring at the front of the house, learn more about Montague Howe and, most importantly, learn why he, Kent, had been so deviously lured to this place. That, however, might be dangerous. On the other hand, continuing to dwell upon Howe's chicanery stoked his stubbornness to the flashpoint.

And when an angry Hebrides baron becomes stubborn, only death will swerve him from his chosen path.

"Like hell," he told the lizard. "As Joe Bill might say, 'I may be dumb but I ain't stupid.' "

A finger tapped his shoulder.

Immediately, one hand grabbed the railing to prevent him from pitching over while the other one grabbed at his chest and just barely managed to keep his heart from scrambling outside his rib cage.

"Jesus H!" he snapped, and spun around angrily. "Joe Bill, what the bloody hell—"

Bambi Howe, crimson lips and emerald eyes, smiled up at him coyly. "Did I startle you, Baron?"

Her blonde hair had been teased, tempted, and whipped into dancing curls and bouncy ringlets that teased the tops of bare shoulders that rose sensuously above a fluffed, puffed, lacy, hoop-skirted pastel green dress; the waist was narrow, the neckline ridiculous, the effect so intense Kent knew instantly Rhett never would have made it up the stairs if Scarlett had had the same seamstress.

As the red fan she held in her right hand fluttered before her face, she did a slow turn so that he could see her back. Lots of it.

The lizard jumped.

"Ah hope," she said demurely as the fan delicately descended to the round of her bosom, "y'all haven't been so lonely up here that you would mistake me for a common chauffeur."

As he searched for a voice that wouldn't crack, gasp, or do anything more than grunt, he told her with a smile and an apologetic nod that no one in his right mind would ever mistake her for a chauffeur, common or not.

Her fan accepted the apology and suggested that he didn't look half bad himself.

His posture was grateful for the compliment, it was just a little something he threw together on the spur of the moment, and hoped he wouldn't embarrass her and her family in front of their honored guests.

The fan fluttered that such a thing was surely impossible, and it was she who would be most honored if he found the time to have at least one dance with her before this too-short evening ended.

A gesture inquired after her sister.

The fan told him what he could do with her sister.

A twitch of his lips denied having done anything like that before, on any continent.

A playful burble in her throat suggested merriment and promise.

An animal's agonized scream deep in the swamp interrupted the conversation.

"Nothing to fear, sir," she said calmly, stepping closer. "We hear that sort of thing all the time at night. It's the way of the bayou."

"I see."

She batted her eyelashes at him. "I'm sure you do."

He didn't believe she'd done that.

She did it again.

Faint music drifted from the open windows below.

The sun continued to drop, thickening the shadows between the trees to make them seem like a semisolid wall. Someone inside threw a switch and the Chinese lanterns flared on. Footsteps on the veranda below signaled the languid flow of guests.

The fan rapped his chest playfully.

"Silly me," she declared. "I just don't know what's come over me, sir. I have completely forgotten the reason for my visit to your quarters."

"I thought it was to see me," he suggested with a chuckle.

The fan tapped his arm.

"Well, of course, Kent—may I call you Kent? we're not terribly formal down here as you can see—Kent, I've come to introduce you to my daddy."

He mouthed *ah,* and gaped when, suddenly, she uttered a small scream and flung herself at him. He embraced her, looked around for assassins—his mother had always had the goddamn worst timing—predator hawks, fanged snakes, and could see only the lizard puffing back to the railing.

He grinned. "It's only a wee lizard," he said.

She muttered something into his chest.

A finger under her chin tilted her face to his, and a look asked her to repeat what she'd just said.

"I hate them," she said, shuddering. "They have—forgive me for being such a child—they have terrible associations in my memory."

"Well, then," he said, escorting her into the sitting room and opening the door with a flourish, "why don't we just go downstairs and meet your father? Besides, the little bloke meant you no harm."

"No, they never do, at first," she answered mysteriously.

Kent thought of Wandalina LeJermina; he thought of Silas Bouquette watching at the train station; he thought of Zergopha; he thought of Della Depew when, at the head of the grand staircase, he saw her in the hall below, walking into the front room with a pink balloon in a white suit.

"Well, what do you know, that's our mayor," Bambi said proudly, taking his arm as they began their descent.

"And the woman?"

She huffed a lofty dismissal. "A common slut, that's all." She hugged his arm much too tightly for his blood pressure. "What Daddy calls a necessary evil."

"A slut is a necessary evil?"

"A nurse, silly. She's a nurse, too."

"Ah."

The chandelier was lit, candles flickered in brass sconces, and music filled the air. At the door stood a man easily a head taller than Kent, easily three hundred well-packed pounds, and dressed in silver-and-black livery. He greeted the guests stiffly, his white-gloved hand directing them to the right.

"Henry Fleuret," Bambi said. "A janitor."

"What?"

The fan covered her lips as she tittered. "He's the janitor at the clinic, but when we have these little get-togethers with our close and dear friends, he serves as butler as well. His wife's our cook."

Two for the price of one, he thought; what's wrong with this picture?

When they reached the hall Bambi immediately steered him around the staircase and into the side corridor. Laughter followed them, and the wasp-buzz of conversation, the clink of glasses, the tuning-up of a banjo.

"Tell me," he said, "are you going to be in your father's movie?"

"What movie?"

He frowned, told himself he should have known better the way things were going, but he didn't have anything to lose by giving it the old college try, did he? So he did. And he lost. What the hell, he hadn't been so hot in college either. And he really ought to stop asking that damn question.

They stopped at a paneled oak door.

"The library," she announced.

"Your father," he said.

"Inside," she told him.

I don't want to do this, he thought.

She kissed the side of his chin, kissed his cheek, kissed his earlobe. "Of course," she whispered, the fan patting the back of his neck, "there are sluts and there are sluts."

He coughed.

She giggled.

And opened the door.

Roger Ace, exhausted and hot, impatiently adjusted the sopping sweatband around his head, plucked at the shirt clinging wetly and tightly to his chest, and regripped the oars that had, thus far, given him more splinters than a bare-assed slide down the banister of life.

"I thought," he said with forced cheer, "this thing had a motor."

Timmy, kneeling at the bow with a baseball bat over his shoulder, said, "It did."

"Well, it doesn't now."

The boy shrugged. "Silas said it did. He told me. Didn't he tell me, Momma? Didn't he tell me he got a boat that has a motor on it?"

Bessy Lou, kneeling on the stern seat with a shotgun in her hands, said, "Timmy, I only know what you told me, and that was that Silas had a boat with a motor on it."

"See?" Timmy said.

Roger's parting of the lips might have been construed as a smile were it viewed by a dead man, but even in *Dungeon Rats of the Io Apiary* he hadn't killed off the obnoxious little brat who had, through miscommunication and sweet innocence, nearly destroyed the known universe. So he forbore further criticism lest it be misunderstood by the boy's mother, and pulled on the oars again, and the boat inched forward again, and yet again a clump of Spanish moss slapped him across the back of the head. He didn't move. He didn't complain. He told himself that he was a man, that this sort of physical labor was something a man had to do in order to impress the hell out of the woman he loved and get them all safely home again, but he did have the distinct feeling he was never going to be able to type again. Or sit straight. Or stand with any conviction whatsoever. Rowing was hard; hell, it was hell.

If it hadn't been for the impressive shattered egg he had

seen in the unnerving nest the boy had led them to, he would have taken one of the oars and rung the changes on the kid's thick skull.

"Roger, are you thinking?"

"Yes," he answered, tone surly.

Something of a decent size dove into the water a few yards away, the ripples as dark as the swamp's oily surface; a hawk swooped into a tree, and out again with something wriggling and squealing in its beak.

Roger speeded up a notch.

"Are you thinking that Timmy could be right and Zergopha has returned to demolish our homes and families?"

"In a way," he answered.

And in a way he was also thinking about Bessy Lou's father, a young man at the time of the last monster sighting, a young man out fishing in the bayou, a young man who had seen the creature, and instead of warning Howe's Landing of its imminent doom, had drunk himself into an incoherent stupor at one of the town bars. Roger himself didn't think such a reaction was all that terrible, considering the fact there were supposed to have been two of the things at the time; but towns will talk, and towns will point a collective finger, and towns that get ravaged will have to have a scapegoat who, in this case, happened to be out of his alcoholic mind at the time.

The rest is history.

A bird called harshly, another answered the bold challenge; a huge yellow-and-red snake slipped across the water and swallowed a bloated toad sunning itself on a mossy hillock.

Roger found another notch and cranked it.

Timmy turned around, an earnest look on his little freckled face. "So, are we gonna hunt it down and kill it, Roger, huh? Are we gonna stay out all night with torches and things until we find it so that Momma can blast it to perdition?"

"Timmy!" gasped Bessy Lou.

"Not on your life, son," Roger managed between increasingly large drops of sweat and a heartfelt grunt.

"Aw."

The scream of a hungry panther echoed through the cypress, and something else jumped into the water with a strangled gurgle; gas bubbled beneath a floating island of grass; a beautiful avian melody echoed in the distance; an elephant trumpeted; reeds rustled; an alligator coughed.

It was getting altogether too full of nature around here for Roger's comfort, and he redoubled his efforts to ride the row-boat on its bow.

"We'll have to tell the sheriff," Bessy Lou decided.

"Sure," Roger said sourly.

"And the mayor."

"Right."

"And Doc Pruit will have to get the clinic ready for casualties."

"Sure."

"Don't forget the militia, Momma," Timmy said as he knocked a cottonmouth into right field.

"Got it," said Roger.

"Perhaps," Bessy Lou added pensively, "we should ride into the back country and warn folks like the Fleurets. They don't get TV, how are they going to know about Zergopha?"

"Good," Roger muttered.

And while we're at it, we'll call the National Guard, the network news people, the governor, maybe even the Russians, who supposedly know about these things, and tell them we've got a zillion-year-old monster that just hatched from a large blue egg, and it's going to kill us all in our beds. It would make a hell of a book, but one hell of a lousy phone call.

A vulture watched them blandly as they passed beneath its perch.

"Are we there yet?" Timmy asked.

Roger looked over his shoulder. And frowned. He didn't know. As far as he was concerned, one part of the bayou looked like any other part in spite of his writer's trained eyes for detail. They could be in Missouri for all he knew. Besides, he thought Bessy Lou was doing the navigating.

"Bessy Lou, are you doing the navigating?" he asked as his shirt finally split down the back.

"Well, Roger, how would I know? I was depending on Timmy to get us back, since he's already familiar with the country."

Timmy looked up from bashing a water lily. "Say what?"

Roger looked at the boy; he felt Bessy Lou looking at him; Timmy looked at his bat and said, "If we get lost, can I make a fire in the boat to keep away the gators so they don't eat us until we die?"

The library was filled with books, chairs, tables for drinks, a grand piano with a Spanish shawl draped over it, a harp in the far corner beside a stuffed bear, the heads of elk and moose over a fireplace large enough to fry Kent's mother in.

Montague Howe stood on the hearth, a dog panting by his feet.

Bambi bounced in, announced Kent, bounced out, bounced back in and told them not to be stick-in-the-muds, because people were just dying to meet their very first baron, bounced out again, and bounced back apologetically to say that Matilda Fleuret absolutely insisted that dinner be on time for a change because she'd spent all day slaving over a hot stove and she didn't care if Kent Montana was the King of England, done was done and don't anyone be late.

"That's a quote," she added, blushing. "I didn't mean to offend you, Kent, if I did, but that's the way we talk down here, plain and simple, makes no never mind who."

"I noticed," he said.

She bounced out.

He waited.

The door remained closed.

"Mr. Montana, at last we meet."

Discipline, son, discipline, Kent told himself as he crossed the huge room and shook Howe's hand. He noted how powerful the man's grip was, took the offered armchair, and crossed his legs as he folded his hands in his lap.

Howe remained on the hearth.

Ah, Kent realized; the clever devil's staying there while I'm sitting here so he'll be able to look down on me and I'll have to look up at him, thus placing him in a position of psychological power.

"So," he said without preamble, "what about this movie?"

"What movie?" Howe said.

Damn.

Howe smiled then, and bowed his head in sheepish apology so blatantly insincere the mastiff slobbered with joy. "I truly must apologize for the perpetuated ruse, Mr. Montana, but you

must not blame your agent. He is without guilt. It is entirely my
own fault."

Kent said nothing.

"But you see, sir, it was the only way I could think of to get
someone of your caliber and importance down to a small town
like this to help a small businessman like myself out of what
we call around here a dill of a pickle."

He chuckled.

Kent wondered how many punches he could get in before that
dog tore off his arm.

"I will, of course, make it well worth your while."

Maybe if he got the dog first, with that poker over there, and
then went for the man . . .

"It's a project I do believe a gentleman of your background
will be fascinated by."

Kent saw it then, and mentally slapped himself silly for not
seeing it before—the Bayou Blast. Use his name, his title, and
if possible not a little of his fortune to convince whoever it was
who needed convincing that the Blast was well and truly the best
thing that would ever happen to this town. It wouldn't matter
that along the way a way of life would be destroyed, homes
bulldozed under, and families scattered all the way to Tulsa; it
wouldn't matter that only a few people would actually prosper
from this venture.

It wouldn't matter at all as long as Montague Howe got his
sodding cut.

Of course, if he was wrong he'd feel like an idiot.

"I'm sure," Howe continued, idly slapping the crop against
his leg, "that you've seen sign of, or have heard about, something called the Bayou Blast?"

Kent nodded, his expression so powerfully noncommittal that
it seemed to make the plantation owner uneasy.

"And I'm sure you know that I am privileged to be one of
the primary backers."

Bingo.

Kent examined his fingernails, the backs of his hands, the
crease of his trousers. "And this . . . problem?"

"People."

"People?"

"They don't want it."

"Who doesn't want it?"

"People."

"Ah."

"And it was my humble suggestion to the others who are, shall we say, more progressive than some, that we call upon the services of a man who is not only a distinguished member of the royal family in extension, but also a consummate actor." He paused for a reaction, received none, smiled again. "Such a powerful combination in one man revered and respected by all who know him would surely win the day for us, the Blast, Howe's Landing, and the great State of Louisiana.

A smattering of applause filtered into the room.

"Mr. Montana, are you listening to me?"

Kent blinked. "Not really, no."

Howe stiffened, the smile was swallowed, and his eyes narrowed. "Mr. Montana, as you can well imagine, I am not used to being spoken to like that."

Kent uncrossed his legs, drew a hand over his mouth, and stood. "And I, Mr. Howe, am not used to being conned, tricked, lied to, and otherwise treated like an ignorant fool." At least not in Louisiana, he amended. He took a step toward the fireplace. The mastiff rose. "And if that beast so much as looks at me cross-eyed, I'll belt him with that fucking bear."

Howe's face reddened.

Thor slobbered in anticipation.

"My project," Howe finally managed.

"Sod your project," Kent spat with contempt. "If you want to build a goddamn playground for gullible tourists and milk the town dry while you're at it, you can do it without my help, whatever the hell you thought that might consist of." He jabbed a finger at the dog; Thor sat; Howe gaped. "I've been warned about you in one way or another since the moment I set foot in this state, and the only thing I'm sorry for is that I didn't listen to any of them." He marched to the door, opened it, and turned around. "I am going to have dinner, I am going to pack, I am going to have Mr. Spain drive me to town where I'm sure I'll be able to locate accommodations until such time as I am able to hire transportation to the nearest airport."

He stepped out into the hallway, congratulated himself, then poked his head back in.

"And I still think it's bloody stupid to name a woman after a goddamn deer."

He slapped the door.

"God!" he said, threw up his hands, and turned.

And bumped into a woman in a blue dress so simple it was obscene. She held a cup of coffee in her hand which, without apology, he grabbed and drank, sighing loudly in startled delight at its curious but invigorating punch.

"Chicory," she said.

"Pleased to meet you. Kent Montana."

She turned her head to look at him sideways. "Is that a joke?"

He took another drink. "Well, actually, that's not my real name, but it serves me in my career, such as it was. You wouldn't like my real name. Hell, you wouldn't believe my real name. I like Montana. It has a ring to it that something like Wisconsin definitely lacks."

"My god, you're not joking."

He was confused, and so took yet another drink that emptied the cup.

"Della Depew," she said.

"Yes," he said. "I know."

"You do?"

He smiled. "Your reputation precedes you." And laughed. "I'm very pleased to meet you."

They shook hands; her grip was powerful yet gentle, strong without cracking his knuckles, yet tender enough to engender decidedly unbaronlike tingles in several regions he'd thought long since permanently deadened by the train ride. Then he heard a snarling behind the closed library door, took Della's arm, and led her toward the front.

She did not object.

"Are you really a baron?" she asked.

"To my mother's constant dismay, yes. And are you really not only a bartender but a nurse as well?"

"When I have to be," she said with a quiet laugh that made him smile inside as well as out. "There's a clinic here where I work, but only when there's a patient." Her smile was rueful and one sided. "You may have noticed that there isn't exactly a metropolitan population in the Landing. And what populace there is doesn't need me as much as I'd wish." She patted his arm and steered him toward the doors to the front room. "So what are you doing here?"

The room, high ceilings and gold trim, flocked red velvet walls and royal blue carpeting, was filled without crowding, and there was a constant flow through an arched entrance to the ballroom beyond. A few people glanced at him, dismissed him, and continued their conversations, most of which, he surmised, had to do with either raising money, pigs, children, or hell.

And as he strolled with Della toward the French doors opening onto the side veranda, he explained how he had been duped, lured into visiting Howe's Landing under pretext of making a film which would revive his sagging career, how he had lost his temper with the sanctimonious Howe only a few minutes ago, and how he was going to enjoy himself while he could because dawn would see him no more substantial around here than summer and smoke.

"Ah," she said, "so the sweet bird of youth flies the coop and leaves behind all the fine young—"

She stopped.

He looked at her, and realized with a silent groan that she was studying him intently, moving her head side to side as if to get a better view, though the only way she could do that would be to sit in his lap.

No, he thought in abrupt panic. He knew that look. No, please, not here, not now. He scanned the room for someone, anyone, to interrupt them.

"Hey!" Her lips parted. "Hey!"

Damn.

"I know you."

"Yes, we've just met. Out in the hall. You have a good memory."

"Very funny. But I *know* you, damnit." She scowled in concentration. She sucked her upper lip between her teeth. She bent down as if to get an upward angle on his chin. She tapped her finger on her chin before pointing it at him. "You didn't talk like that, though. When I saw you."

"Like what?" He didn't have to ask. He didn't want to ask.

"Like the way you push your *r*'s around. Like a Scot, y'know?"

"I am a Scot."

"But you weren't."

"Tell that to my mother. No, never mind. She thinks I'm in Moscow."

She snapped her fingers.

Shit, he thought.

"Why, sure! Hot damn! You were a butler, right? On *Passions and Power*, right?" She applauded herself in delight. "I used to watch you every day before the tube in the bar blew. I got the damn thing fixed, you were gone. Some other guy was there, a little fat guy with a white mustache."

"My replacement," he said stiffly.

Her expression sobered. "I got a feeling y'all didn't retire."

Despite the pain, despite the melancholy that rose in his artistically agonized breast, despite the anguished howling of outrageous fortune outside the window of his soul, he allowed as how she was right.

"Too bad," she said sympathetically. "You did good."

"Thank you." And then, suddenly, he took her arm and looked toward the center hall. "Yes," he said quietly. "Thank you indeed."

Puzzled, she tried to see what he was looking at. "I'm sorry, I don't understand."

"He was lying," Kent said, speaking as much to himself as he was to her. "The bastard was lying." A smile that never made it to his eyes. "Miss Depew, how would you like to go with me?"

"Where?"

"To find a monster."

"No thanks," she said, "I already know the mayor."

·2·

Roger staggered up Poppy Lane, Bessy Lou supporting him on one side, Timmy skipping ahead, swinging the baseball bat at imagined monsters that tried to ambush them from behind every shrub and hedge, every vine and weed. By the time they reached the clinic, Roger was ready to kill him.

It was, in point of fact, humiliating to be practically carried up the walk by a schoolteacher and her son; it was downright disgraceful the way she had to open the door for him because his hands were swollen with blisters wherever the splinters hadn't taken root; and it was damned ignominious when they stepped over the threshold and the act of lifting his legs caused such agony in his rowing-bent spine that he had to bite back a scream and bit his tongue instead.

"Hello!" Bessy Lou called.

There was no answer.

He tottered into the reception room and dropped onto the couch with a groan.

"Hello?" Bessy Lou offered as she made her way back toward the emergency examining room.

Timmy, in graphic and high-pitched detail, knocked off the head of an attacking creature by the window.

Roger glared at him.

Humiliating.

Heroes, he thought, do not need splinters yanked from their heroic hands, for God's sake.

Bessy Lou returned in a state of mild agitation. "He's not here," she announced. "Timmy, hush now, your momma's trying to talk. I don't know where he is."

Roger closed his eyes and leaned back. "The party," he said wearily. "I'll bet he's gone to the Manor."

Bessy Lou stamped a foot in frustration. "Of course! How stupid of me to forget."

Timmy swung at an invasion of monsters, missed, and chipped out a fair chunk of Blanche Knox's desk.

Roger ordered himself some spunk and a side dish of grit, and checked his hands. "I think you can handle the splinters, Bessy. There must be something in there you can use."

"Timmy, darling, let's not forget we're not supposed to play in someone else's house."

Timmy separated the Steuben penguin from its base as he vanquished another foe.

"I think I can get away with just bandaging the blisters."

Bessy Lou seemed doubtful.

Roger urged her with a smile to fetch the tweezers and some gauze and tape.

She hurried away.

He pushed himself to the edge of the cushion, ducked the bat, and grabbed Timmy's arm. The pain was neatly absorbed by the sudden expression of anxiety in the boy's face.

"Knock it off," Roger said flatly.

"But Roger!"

"You swing that thing one more time, son, and I'll fix it so you'll never be able to sit again without a pillow, a rubber ring, and a diaper."

The boy's eyes widened.

Roger's eyes narrowed.

The bat dropped to the floor.

"Thank you, Roger," Bessy said from the doorway. "I've always said he needs a man's influence at times like these." She jerked her head to direct her son into the nearest chair. "And if you move," she added sweetly, "Roger will kill you."

The boy gaped.

Roger gaped.

Roger gasped when, in swift succession, blisters were bandaged, splinters were removed, iodine was applied, gauze was wrapped, and tape was secured. He hardly had time to scream more than once before she rocked back onto her heels and grinned in self-satisfaction.

And the door banged open.

"God damn!" Doc Pruit yelled hoarsely as he rushed in. "Wouldn't you know I'd forget my own damned belt! Jesus Christ, some day I'll forget my what the hell are you people doing in my clinic?"

Roger held up his hands.

Doc frowned and came closer. "Christ, son, what the hell happened to you?"

"Zergopha," Timmy said in a small voice.

Doc staggered sideways until he came up against the desk. "You're kidding."

"It's true," Roger told him. "In a way."

"What way is that?"

"We found the nest."

"Oh dear Lord."

Bessy Lou, making full use of her lecturing skills, described their exploratory trip, their harrowing escape from the dangerous wilds of the wilderness, and the makeshift emergency methods she used to safeguard Roger's invaluable typing hands before all manner of infection, feculence, gangrene, and other nasty communicable symptoms robbed him of the only means he had to support his new family.

"Jesus," Roger whispered, and felt faint.

Doc, fairly respectable in his Sunday best brown suit minus the belt, walked around the desk several times before Roger, sensing something was more amiss than the simple arrival of a legendary monster, asked him what was wrong.

"Wrong?" Pruit asked, voice rising, blood rising, rising himself. "Wrong? Well, hell's bells, what could be wrong? I've only let things go too far, that's all. I've only put the entire town, the whole state, and probably the whole damn country in mortal jeopardy, that's what's wrong!" He brought a fist down onto the blotter. "And I can't stand by a second longer, party or no party." He pointed at them. "You stay here. I have something to show you."

At that moment the door slammed inward and three disheveled and bloodied teenagers stumbled into the reception room.

"Zergopha!" Jacques Fleuret cried.

A bugle sounded on Main Street.

"I know, I know," Doc grumbled as he hastened into the emergency room.

"He knows?" Jonelle Fleuret said to Bessy Lou.

The teacher nodded.

Jacques sat on the floor where he stood, too dazed to say anything.

Louisa buried a hand in her hair. "You mean to tell me we run all this way through the damn swamp to warn you people about that thing out there and you already know about it?" She slapped Jacques across the back of his head. "You hear that? They already know about it!"

Timmy grabbed up the bat. "And Roger almost lost our only weapon, too."

"I did not almost lose it," Roger huffed. "I was trying to save us from a hungry alligator."

"It was dead."

"Forgive me, but I did not think to ask about its physical condition when those damn vultures dropped it on my head," the writer snapped.

"I had to dive in and get it," Timmy said proudly.

Bessy Lou slapped him across the back of his head and told him to hush.

Pruit returned and dropped a stack of papers on the desk. "Not only do I know about it," he said ominously, "I was the one who helped bring it to life."

Jonelle burst into tears and demanded to know where her father was.

"At the Manor," the doctor said as Roger, unable to contain himself, hurried to the desk and began to read the first page. "I gave him the day off so he could help your mother cook or something."

"I want him here!" Jonelle begged hysterically through her tears. "I want him now! I want him here! I want—"

Louisa slapped her.

Jonelle dropped to her knees and covered her face with her hands.

Jacques absently brought Louisa to the floor as well by clocking her knee with the shotgun stock, then turned to Bessy Lou and said, "Miss Leigh, as far as I can tell, Zergopha is heading for the Manor."

Bessy Lou demanded to know how he could know this.

He told her about the wholesale killing of his uncle, the wanton destruction of their just-painted home, the flight along the rutted road until the damn truck had a flat tire. Plus, he had seen it himself, making its way northward through the swamp. That could only mean one thing.

Roger, already on page twenty-three, said without looking up, "Actually, it could mean it was lost. Jesus, Doc, you mean you actually made an omelet?"

"Tastes like chicken," Pruit replied.

"Sonofabitch."

"Roger," scolded Bessy Lou.

"Sorry."

"I gotta pee," Timmy sniffled.

"Cross your legs," Roger muttered crossly. "This is more important."

The bugle sounded again, and they all looked to the window and realized with a start that twilight had replaced sunlight, the streetlights had come on, and a faint mist had begun to creep along the ground.

The world had turned black and white.

Myrtle Mae watched as Gert scooted on down the sidewalk, heading for the depot to check for the monster.

She checked Ethel June, standing on the roof of the General Store and Notion Parlor, trying to dump the spit from her bugle.

She checked her bowie knife by swinging at a bee, and when it buzzed off unharmed, she told herself not to worry. Nerves. It was nothing but nerves, nothing to get all jumped up about, just mind your instructions to the troops and everything will be all right.

Ethel June blew again.

Gert returned to report that all was quiet on the southern flank.

Quiet, thought Myrtle Mae.
Just the way she liked it.

Silas Bouquette just happened to glance out the window of
his shack while on the way to the stove to give a stir to the
sorghum-and-franks he was heating up. What he saw out by
the wreckage of the chicken coop stopped him in midstride.
His good leg trembled. His bad leg felt nailed to the floor. His
stomach tumbled the beans he'd just eaten. His blood fermented
the liquor he'd had with Rude before heading home to change
clothes so he could meet the stationmaster back in town for the
more serious and lengthy portion of their Friday night drinking.
His throat felt raw. His eyes struggled not to see what they saw.
His hands clenched, unclenched, and clenched again.

His gun was nowhere in sight.

"Damn," he whispered. "All this time sitting at the depot, I
could've stayed home."

It was more than a shadow, less than a clear vision of a creature slightly taller than a man, walking on two trunk-thick legs
covered with gleaming triangular scales whose color was lost in
the dimming glow of twilight. Its feet, when it bent over to clear
a squashed but still wriggling serpent from between its clawed
toes, were splayed and webbed; its back was broad, a row of
long red feathers rippling down its spine; its arms were as thick
as its legs, and again, covered with scales; and its head was,
at the same time, that of a man with a red-feather wig, and an
alligator that had just scalped a man with a red-feather wig.

It stopped.

Silas whimpered.

Ponderously its head swiveled around, and he saw the slanted
gold eyes, the blunt snout, the double row of teeth when it opened
its lipless mouth, the serpentine tongue that flicked at the air.

It looked at him.

Silas looked back.

It raised its clawed hands and roared, bellowed, howled,
wailed, bawled, and screamed before, suddenly, slipping away
into the dark.

Silas looked at the ceiling and thanked the good Lord and
the memory of his granddaddy for sparing his life and allowing
him not to soil the only decent pair of pants he had in the house

since the others were in the cleaners, then lunged for the telephone, dropped the receiver, picked it up, dropped it again, stood panting until he could control his hands, lunged for the receiver and trapped it between his jaw and shoulder while he dialed a number and stared at the ghost of Zergopha, still lingering out there at the edge of his property, telling him that as soon as it was finished with present business it was going to return and tear him apart.

A voice answered.

"Custard," he said shakily.

"What?" Myrtle Mae said. "That you, Silas?"

"Custard," he repeated desperately.

"Good lord, you brought me all the way in here from my guard post doing my duty, you know how hot it is, you idiot, just to tell me custard?"

"Well, ain't that the damn code word?" he snapped.

"Silas, you drinking again?"

"Not damn near enough, Myrtle. So you gonna custard or what?"

"But I'm already ready, fool. Ain't you heard Ethel June's bugle? Hell, her dentures nearly clipped a seven-aught-seven not ten minutes ago."

"I saw him."

There was a contemplative pause.

"How do you know?"

"I'm the Watcher, I gotta know these things."

There was another pause.

"What'd he look like?"

"Uglier than Joe Bill."

"Oh my god, Silas, that's him all right."

There was an alarmed silence.

"He's heading for the Manor."

"Shoot."

"Can't find my gun."

"No, fool, not that shoot. The other shoot."

He waited.

"Poor Gert, she can't get to the Manor, her walker being the way it is. She's gonna just hate missing the kill."

Silas checked the window again. "Myrtle Mae, there ain't gonna be no kill."

"What?"

"Not unless Zergopha's doing it."

"But my bowie knife—"

"Myrtle Mae, I seen what I seen and there ain't nothing in this world gonna stop that critter less than one of those atomic bomb things we saw on PBS last spring."

"Damn."

Then Silas gasped.

"Silas?"

He dropped the receiver.

"Hey, Silas, you there?"

He turned to run just as Zergopha exploded through the floor-boards from under the house.

He screamed.

Myrtle Mae screamed.

And Zergopha, incredibly, laughed.

·3·

Brilliantly feathered birds cried warnings to each other.

Reptiles of all sizes slapped the water with their tails, grunted, coughed, hissed, and swam in instinctive panic for the deepest, darkest interiors of the bayou.

Mammals scrambled up gnarled trees, dove into warm burrows, froze under protective-coloration bushes and tried frantically not to tremble.

Unclassifiable creatures sought refuge in trenches, deserted nests, ruins of civilizations long ago lost, skeletons rotting in shallow open graves.

And then, suddenly, the swamp was silent.

Too silent.

Not a leaf rustled, not an insect buzzed, not a ripple splashed, not a breeze blew, not a twig snapped.

Zergopha reared onto its legs and sniffed the air.

It nodded.

It picked its teeth with its claws, spat out a few chunks of wood, and tested the air again.

The time was right.

A moment later the clearing was deserted, nothing left but a few pitifully small bones, and a scrap of still-bleeding red meat.

Only the shadows moved.

-V-

Howe's Bayou

⋆ 1 ⋆

A delicate, not uncomfortable chill settled over the plantation with the setting of the sun, bringing many couples to the veranda, to the yard, as they awaited the feast being prepared for them in the dining room. Kent, however, ignored most of it save for a marvelously structured blonde in a white sequined dress being escorted by a man in a white rawhide-fringed jacket trimmed in red.

"Wally Torn, the sheriff," Della whispered. "The other one is Blanche. She works at the clinic."

"Doing what?"

"Anything she wants to."

Kent didn't ask.

Della didn't elaborate.

The sheriff nodded politely to him, Blanche batted her eyelashes at him, and several men collided with the ornate posts holding up the roof.

"Do you Southern women always do that?" he asked.

"Do what?"

He batted his eyelashes at her. "That."

She laughed, hiccupped, laughed again so hard he had to slip an arm around her waist to keep her from falling over. "Sorry," she gasped, and laughed again. They passed the open doors to the ballroom. "God, I am sorry," she sputtered, and brayed. Kent glanced in and saw a number of guests standing in front of a raised platform set against the far wall. "Damn," she sighed, and kept it down to a roar.

Kent decided batting was no skill a well-meaning baron should acquire.

Della straightened, composed herself, and grinned. "Sorry."

"It's quite all right."

Her cheeks were flushed, her lips a brighter red, her hair mussed without being unbrushed. Suddenly he had an almighty urge to take her into an informal embrace and kiss the living lips off her, and it must have shown in his eyes and the way his hands twitched, because she looked away quickly and said, with a nod, "That's Herman Quillborn."

He followed her look, and saw a short, portly man in a battered tuxedo, who not only obviously didn't get an instructional note but also just as obviously had a silver instrument bolted to his leg. He was seated on a small portable stage and speaking jovially to a group of people standing in front of him.

Kent couldn't understand a word he was saying.

"He comes from Alabama," the nurse explained.

"With that banjo on his knee?" He also couldn't understand, once the playing resumed, how the man's fingers stayed on.

"Industrial accident," she told him. "Apparently it rained all night the day he left, and the weather—"

"Stop," he suggested pleasantly.

She shrugged.

He released her waist, but she grabbed his hand before he could slip it into a pocket. No protest was offered. He liked the feeling, enjoyed the idea of a private nurse who knew how to pour a good drink, and realized when they reached the back that their posture fit in rather well with the other couples now strolling through the gardens or sitting at the tables being served by a small army of white-jacketed waiters carrying trays loaded with champagne.

They stepped down to the grass and paused.

"Where are we going?"

He lifted his chin in the direction of the fieldstone wall. "Back there."

"Why?"

"Do you really want to know?"

"Only if it's the mayor you're looking for."

His laugh was genuine; it made him feel good. "What is it about the mayor that has you so crackling?"

"He wants my land," she said simply, taking the first step and forcing him to follow. "For the Blast." She explained about political pressures, personal threats, artificial raising of taxes in order to force her to sell, mysterious letters, mysterious phone calls. "They really can't do it without me."

He didn't have to ask why she wouldn't sell; he could hear it in her voice, and see it in the way she looked at Howe Manor with mild but effective contempt.

"The gentry against the town," he said knowingly.

"Hell no," she said. "He's just an asshole, that's all, and his partner, old Montague, is meaner than cramps."

To that he could attest, and so said nothing more until they reached the fieldstone wall, and its iron gate.

"Locked," Della said.

And the top of the wall, he suspected, had been embedded with glass, sharp stone, wire, explosives, poison darts, or rusty spear tips. Through the gate, however, he could see a narrow path. He stepped closer, but it was too dark to see more than fifty yards or so. He nodded. Back there was the secret place Joe Bill and Wandalina had mentioned. Back there was the real reason he had been brought to Howe Manor.

"Ah wouldn't try it if Ah were you."

They turned quickly.

Arlaine Howe stood on the grass, hands folded demurely at her waist. She wore a dress similar to Bambi's, save hers was a vivid—one might even say sanguine—red, and her dark hair flowed freely. The black choker was stark around her neck despite the diamond glittering coldly at its center. In the dim light, her makeup looked like cracked plaster after an August thunderstorm over the Gulf.

"Alligators," she explained with a terse smile. "They hear the music, they hear the people, they wait for some drunken fool to climb over the wall." The smile vanished. "Mr. Montana, you have offended my father."

"He offended me," Kent replied coldly.

"He is only trying to do his best for Howe's Landing."

Della snorted.

Arlaine glared. "Slut."

"Virgin."

"Ladies, ladies," Kent interjected sternly. "Please, there are guests. I suggest a little decorum, don't you think?"

Arlaine's hands grappled with themselves while her cheeks puffed, collapsed, puffed, collapsed, and a peculiar pulsation bulged behind her choker. Flakes of makeup fluttered to the ground. Kent was positive she was going to attack them, and so braced himself while Della, startled by the transformation, edged behind him.

"I'm a nurse," she whispered when he frowned at her. "Gotta stay alive to attend the wounded."

I am blessed, he thought, and faced the Howe woman squarely, a baron unruffled by the assault of a peasant, an aristocrat unmoved by the posturing of a petty merchant, an actor who has forgotten what play he's in and so stands in arrogant repose until someone else says something first and gives him a clue as to what the hell is going on.

Arlaine calmed.

A dinner gong sounded.

"Mr. Montana, I shall not permit this insult to my family to go unchallenged."

"Your family has a woman named after a deer," he couldn't resist saying.

"My family, *sir*, is a respected, educated, forward-seeing, horizon-drawn unit which shall not, I say shall not be deterred by the verbal garbage spewed by someone as despicably common as you, baron or not."

Kent felt himself grow pale.

Arlaine turned sharply and marched toward the house, pushing aside those who were leisurely heading in for their meal. She did not look back.

The yard grew silent.

Della moved to stand in front of him, admiration in her eyes, and not a little uneasiness. "Is that what barons do?"

He looked down at her.

"Yeah, that's it," she said. "Just like that."

"I cannot help being what I am," he said coldly. Then he

looked toward the house. "And that woman is out of her god-damn mind."

A man waved from the veranda.

Kent squinted, recognized him, and beckoned.

The man waved.

Kent inhaled sharply and beckoned.

The man hesitated.

Della looked, sighed, cupped her hands around her lips, and yelled, "Joe Bill, goddamnit, get your toes on the road and get your buns down here! Can't you see he's pissed?"

Kent looked at her.

She smiled. "We're not very formal down here."

"So I've been told."

Joe Bill, resplendent in a fresh uniform of dark green with gold piping, puffed up to them, his face lightly freckled with sweat. "You drunk, Baron?"

"No," Della said. "But he's madder than hell."

A second gong sounded.

"Mr. Spain," Kent said, "we're going into the swamp."

Joe Bill developed a tic in one eye. "You think that LeJermina was right?"

"I don't know," Kent said as he turned to the gate. "But I'm going to find out."

Bessy Lou clapped her hands angrily, and everyone in the reception room looked at her with a mixture of annoyance and awe. "We can't stay here all night," she declared. "We have to get to the Manor and warn them all."

Roger looked up from Doc Pruit's secret notes. "It may be too late."

"Not if we take the ambulance," the doc said.

Timmy cheered.

Jacques used the Remington to lever himself to his feet. "I'll ride shotgun."

"Why?" Louisa demanded.

"Because I've got the shotgun."

"Well, I've got a spear."

"There ain't no such thing as riding spear."

Louisa admitted defeat.

Doc ducked into the emergency room and returned with a black bag. He opened it and took hasty inventory. "Scalpels, syringes, enough medication to blast a horse into next March. If I can get close enough, we can knock Zergopha out." When they stared in disbelief, he snapped the bag closed. "Hey, I may be a party to death and horrid torture, but I'm still a scientist. If we can study it, we can understand it, and if we can understand it, perhaps we can communicate with it, find out what it wants, what it's good for."

"Bullshit," Roger said.

"Roger," Bessy Lou scolded.

"Yay!" Timmy cheered.

Jonelle sobbed.

"Besides," Roger said solemnly, "we already know what it's good for."

Doc scowled. "Really?"

"Well, it sure don't plant taters."

"And it don't plant cotton," Jacques added.

"And them's that cross it," Louisa said grimly, "are soon forgotten."

Doc looked at them all. "Yes, I suppose you're right. It just keeps rolling."

"Damn right," Roger agreed. "That thing just keeps rolling along, until we smash it forever and save our town."

"Yay!" Timmy cheered.

Bessy Lou smiled. "Well, then. May I suggest we get going?"

The bugle sounded.

Montague Howe remained in the library after the first call to dinner. He fumed. He simmered. He whirled around on the hearth and pointed angrily at his daughter.

"Peaches, damnit, you told me he was an idiot!"

Bambi remained unflustered. "You play a butler when you're really a baron, you got to be an idiot."

Howe glowered. "The man is not an idiot. For all we know, he may already know everything."

"Oh, I don't think so, Daddy." Her smile was frigid. "Not everything."

With an incomprehensible oath he lashed out with the crop

and clipped Thor smartly on the nose. The mastiff growled, whined, and slunk away into a corner.

"We can't lose him, Peaches. Despite everything, he's exactly what we need."

Bambi nodded. "And we will have him, Daddy, don't you worry none about that." A finger tapped her cheek. "All we have to do, we have to keep Arlaine away from him, make sure he doesn't find the lab, and—"

The door opened.

"Hey, Monty," Weatherly greeted. "Thought you was in here. Nice place, real nice, you got a minute to talk to your Blast partner, partner?"

Howe frowned at him. "I'm busy, Stonewall."

The mayor ignored him, instead walked to the nearest table and dropped a hefty package onto it. "Think maybe we could miss the soup if you don't mind, hey, Bambi, but there's something maybe you ought to know about before you set your hired killer on your old partner's ass."

"Hired killer?" Howe said.

"Daddy," Bambi said quietly, "there's something else I got to know."

"That's right," the mayor said, dropping into a chair, looking for all the world like the vulture that ate the lion. "Seems old Doc Pruit didn't destroy those notes of his." He pulled a cigar from his pocket and lit it with a wooden match he struck against his thumbnail. "Kept every word."

Howe stared at the package and saw that it contained many pages wrapped in a bright ribbon whose bow was shoddily done. He shuddered. "Every word," he repeated flatly.

"Daddy, you name me after some critter?"

"Now it seems to me," the mayor said, smiling around the cigar, "that if you call off this hired killer fruit of yours, I don't ever have to let these here papers accidental fall into the wrong hands, of which these papers, by the way so get that look off your face, are a copy and I ain't telling you where or how many others I got."

"I did not hire a killer."

"Oh, of course not," Weatherly said generously. "You just let any old fruit in a blue suit walk in here like he was a baron or something."

"A deer," Bambi said.

Howe smiled without showing his teeth. "Stonewall, you damn fool, the man *is* a baron."

Stonewall puffed, blew smoke toward the ceiling.

"A boy deer."

Thor crawled back to the hearth and ate a log.

"And I suppose," the mayor said through an admirable if not precisely appropriate smoke ring, "he's here to promote and otherwise con folks into believing in the Blast?"

Howe tapped his thigh.

Thor stood up.

"Oh no, Stonewall, he has nothing to do with the Blast."

The mayor was nonplussed and so puffed the cigar again.

"Daddy!"

"Bambi, hooters like them you ain't called after no boy, so shut your trap."

"Daddy!"

"Thor," whispered Howe.

The mastiff grumbled, slapped his tongue around some slobber, and left the hearth.

The mayor became apprehensive and stubbed his cigar out on the table. "Monty, seems like I misjudged you, seems I felt there was something you wasn't telling me when all along you was telling me everything." He laughed—with a tinge of hysteria—when Thor sat in front of him and licked his chops. "Seems like I got the wind up for nothing."

"Hooters?" Bambi said indignantly.

"You read those papers?" Howe asked the mayor.

Weathersly looked at the dog, looked at Howe, looked at the stuffed bear in the corner, and felt sweat break like dawn all over his face.

"Well, Stonewall?"

"Hooters?"

The mayor managed a single nod.

The second gong sounded.

"Dinner," said Howe.

"*Ciao*," said Bambi.

"Please," begged the mayor, just before the mastiff ate.

·2·

It didn't occur to Kent until they were well along the dirt path that perhaps they should have brought along a flashlight, some matches, or some local genius who knew how to make a long-lasting torch from the natural materials at hand. For no sooner had they crossed the first narrow footbridge, under which he could see all manner of fairly indescribable things floating in the dark water with their mouths open, than most of the light faded from the already dim sky. And though he had no doubt that Howe must have some sort of electric generator at this mysterious secret place of his, the getting there in one or more working pieces was going to be rather dicey if they couldn't see where they were going.

"I can't see," Della complained.

A branch, unless it was one of those hanging swamp snakes, brushed across her back and she shrieked quietly, danced backward a few steps, and collided with Kent, who managed an obscure Gaelic oath before grabbing a vine to keep from tumbling into the brush alongside the path.

With no argument from anybody he took the lead.

They traversed another bridge, under which something large but thankfully timid swam in monotonous circles.

Invisible birds cawed and chortled and flapped their wings like the snap of a million shrouds; a cat-thing screamed in apparent frustrated rage; ferns and reeds rustled and crackled in the breeze; that elephant trumpeted again; and if there weren't monkeys chattering and scolding in the high foliage, Kent was an uncle.

"I thought this was a swamp," he muttered.

"You never know in Louisiana," Joe Bill answered as something large flew out of the dark and knocked his new cap into the water. "Damn, gonna get docked for that."

"I can't see," Della grumbled.

A third bridge longer than the others, a fourth less than five paces long, and a fifth so unstable they crossed it one at a time. Della, who had thoughtfully worn pumps to the party instead of her four-inch heels, kicked something squealing out of her way and into the underbrush; Joe Bill swatted through a swarm of insects that seemed bent on nesting in his eyes; Kent paused and wiped a sheen of cold perspiration from his brow before carrying on, studying the writhing shadows, the convoluted boles, the oily surface of the water he could see swirling not six inches below the edge of the path.

Behind them faint, lively music drifted from the mansion ballroom.

At the sixth bridge he called a halt and wiped his face again. On the other side he could see nothing but trees and high brush resting on what seemed to be an island whose banks were little more than exposed roots and stiff reeds.

It was quiet.

The voice of the Louisiana swamp jungle had been hushed.

Kent's mood turned sour. All it needs to be perfect, he thought, is a sign that says *welcome, stupid, to the end of your life*.

Della moved to stand on his right, Joe Bill on his left.

The chauffeur pointed to a canted, weathered post to one side of the bridge. "Used to be a sign here," he said, leaning over and fingering a dark-stained hole. A second later he grunted and held up part of a rusted nail. "Must've fallen off in some storm or other." The iron scrap flipped into the water. "Kind of peculiar, since this road don't fork or anything, why would you need a sign? Can't go anyplace but straight ahead."

"And this trail is pretty old," Della speculated, hiking up her skirt so she could kneel and brush a palm over the ground, sift pebbles between her fingers, touch the tip of her thumb to her mouth as if tasting the earth. "It's hard as rock, been traveled one hell of a long time by a lot of feet." She looked up, puzzled. "But there aren't any fields back this way. Nothing but bayou."

Kent marveled at the uncanny results of their nature-reading skills. Not that they hadn't told him anything he didn't already know, but it was something, he believed, they'd be able to take proudly to their graves and Jesus Christ, Montana, that's a hell of a thing to think now, isn't it.

"Are we going to the other side?" Della wanted to know.

He wished she hadn't put it quite that way.

"We crossing over?" Joe Bill asked.

Or that way, either.

"Perhaps," he said, and used his own actor's skills at keen observation to examine the only access way they had to get to the island.

The hand-wrought structure was at least thirty feet long, with several planks missing. Part of the rope-vine railing dangled over the water, and from the way the bridge quivered in a desultory breeze, he didn't think it would last much beyond the first footstep. He looked down and estimated a ten-foot dive. He slapped a mosquito off the side of his neck. He looked back toward the plantation and wondered how long it would be before Howe realized he was gone and where he was going.

"I vote we get the car," Joe Bill said, his voice low.

We were fools to come out here without weapons, Kent thought, angry at himself for being so thoughtless except for the thought; you lose your temper, you get on your high horse, this is the kind of thing you ride into with your eyes closed and your belly exposed.

Della started across the bridge.

"Hey," he said.

She didn't look back, too busy gamely trying not to fall into the bayou. "I hope you two are coming. I'm going to look awfully stupid otherwise."

Joe Bill sighed loudly and stepped onto the first plank. "I hate women that make men feel like jerks."

"You must be damn lonely," Kent replied as he trailed reluctantly, checking the path behind, the water below, the sky above as it was finally swallowed by the night. He was midway across when something exploded from the swamp and tried to snap his fingers off at the knuckles. He shouted and ducked. The bridge swayed alarmingly, and Della leapt for the far bank and landed on her knees, Joe Bill just behind.

Kent held his breath while the water settled.

He hadn't seen what it was, but it couldn't have been the mythical Zergopha. A creature like that didn't bother trying for the knuckle when it could have the whole hog.

A splash.

He moved again.

Joe Bill and the nurse, indistinct images on the far bank, urged him on with gestures rather than words, some of which Kent believed were altogether too explicit in their opinion of his speed.

The bayou denizen lunged again, just beneath his feet, and he sprang forward as the plank splintered, grabbed the rope-vine rail, and nearly pitched over when the rail parted and he was spun halfway around.

Della yelped.

Joe Bill cursed.

Kent righted himself and waited for his pulse to catch up with his terror; then he moved more nimbly, not daring to look down because he might catch a glimpse of what he was looking for, which sight just might freeze him with terror, thus allowing the hungry beast, whatever the hell it was, another chance to drag him down.

A splash.

A gurgling.

He yelled, leapt for his life, leapt again when he fell short by a yard, and once on the other side was enthusiastically embraced by Della and slapped heartily on the back by the chauffeur; he ignored the enraged thrashing beneath the bridge, thanked his highland gods (and the goddess who lived over the pub in the village) and pressed on.

And stopped five minutes later.

"Aha!" he said.

In a large, uneven clearing dead ahead squatted a low, robust log cabin with a peaked log roof, no porch, and a sturdy generator raised on a platform of logs to one side. Though weeds struggled at the cabin's foundation, the land around it was inexplicably clear of vegetation, and none of the surrounding trees seemed inclined to bend over it. The air was still. Even the insects were absent.

Without giving a word of instruction he approached the building cautiously, Della clinging to one hand, Joe Bill to his shoulder. It was an awkward procession, and most certainly not dignified, but he couldn't blame them. He felt it himself—emanations of evil, intimations of mortality, an aura of that which man was not meant to know, a veritable cloak of suspicion—and dismissed it all out of hand since the other one was crushed in the nurse's powerful grip.

He tried the door.

Ominously, it swung open.

Regrettably, it was dark inside.

When nothing leapt upon his chest and tore out his throat, he reached around the frame and fumbled along the wall until he found a switch.

He flicked it, and a sudden flare of light momentarily blinded them.

From back at the plantation, the single disquieting note of a banjo.

"Aha!" he said again, this time with considerably less verve.

Illumination was provided by four tubular fluorescent bulbs hanging from chains from the rafters, and a handful of flickering Bunsen burners.

After a long interval of indecision during which he took and failed a sanity test, he stepped over the threshold and into a sprawling laboratory the likes of which was bound, he reckoned, to bring tears of righteous envy to the eyes of any non-Defense Department-funded government scientist. Aside from the usual uninspired assortment of test tubes and beakers and bubbling flasks and long tables scored with spilled acid and cages stacked along one wall where once helpless animals had been imprisoned, there was also a fair amount of what he instantly recognized as genetic exploratory instruments, as well as gene-splicing tapes, gene identification tables, Gene Autry records, and gene separation filters. Not to mention the back wall thick with large and small books that ranged from ancient-looking scientific illustrated texts to the most contemporary volumes of scientific speculation and extrapolation.

It was, as far as he could tell, entirely self-contained.

The odd thing was: why hadn't it been locked against intrusion? why was there no alarm system? why could he still hear that infernal banjo playing a dread series of minor, if meaningful, chords?

He didn't like it, neither the music nor the situation. His well-trained sense of preservation, for which he never thought he'd be grateful to his mother and her assassins, set off so many warning bells, he instantly got a headache and had to massage his temples.

"Lord, my medical school wasn't this well equipped," Della said with a bemused shake of her head. "Kent, what *is* the man doing in here?"

Joe Bill coughed, excused himself, coughed again, and wanted to know if anyone wanted to hear the legend and get the warts scared off them.

Kent suggested from his place at the door and his back to the wall that this was the wrong time, not to mention the wrong place, for them to become more unnerved than they already were, but he did provide the nurse with a condensed version of Wandalina LeJermina's story.

"You've got to be kidding," she said. She wandered through the spacious but space-cramped room. "You've really got to be kidding." She opened a small refrigerator, closed it, checked one of the many laden shelves attached to the walls, flipped open a few ledgers and read a few pages, exclaimed over a leather-bound set of medical books she thought only the largest universities owned, ran back to the refrigerator and opened it, leaned in, leaned back and exhaled noisily.

"I'll be damned."

Joe Bill joined her and peered over her shoulder. "Well, she sure got that part right, didn't she."

Della nodded.

Kent remained by the door. He did not care what was in the refrigeration unit, nor did he care what was in the ledgers, nor did he care about the curious boxes on all the shelves, nor did he care about the cages queerly empty of their captives. *This* was what it all boiled down to, *this* was what losing control had bestowed upon him, and he resolved that as long as he didn't care, and didn't know, and didn't learn and therefore did not become knowledgeable, then nothing could harm him except that creature under the last bridge. On the other hand, the one that wasn't still smarting from Depew's nursely grip, his intellectual curiosity was slyly urging him to take that one small step toward his companions, ask that one insignificant what-could-it-hurt question, take a peek at that one miserable little dish Della held up to him. What the hell.

"What is it?" he asked, and kicked the wall for being so weak.

"An egg," Della said, bringing the dish over to the nearest lab table.

He looked, and kicked the wall again.

The egg was twice as large as an ambitious chicken's, pale blue and red, and not quite oval. When he picked it up, hefted it, held it to one ear and shook it lightly, he presumed that there was nothing inside, a supposition supported, he noted, by a small hole in one end.

"I would guess," she guessed, "that it's a failed experiment."

"How right you are, Miss Depew," said Montague Howe from the doorway. "It's a shame you'll never be able to tell anyone about it."

·3·

The ambulance wailed around the corner on two wheels, and barreled straight down the center of the road that led toward Howe Manor.

In the back, too many people to mention individually prepared their weapons and themselves.

✦ 4 ✦

"And this," said Montague Howe with sinister yet restrained glee, "is the tasty little moment, as my darlin' daughter might say, where you tell me with pious indignation and stiff upper lip that I shall never get away with it, that the authorities are on the way, that you've left a damning letter with your banker, which must be opened at a certain time if you do not send him a coded message." He put his hands on his hips, threw back his head, and laughed.

Kent said, "Damn."

He was securely tied to the first lab table, his arms extended awkwardly above his head and his wrists lashed painfully to the corners, the rest of him wrapped three or four times around with rope of near-hawser quality. Spread-eagled as he was, he supposed it could have been worse; he could be on an altar on a South Pacific island, prepared as a human sacrifice to the blue crab god.

Howe laughed again.

Joe Bill and Della, for their part securely tied back to back and plopped unceremoniously onto the second table, merely groaned, since they had also been securely gagged with strips of cloth torn from Kent's coat after it had been, in turn, torn from his back.

Thor woofed in the doorway.

Howe, his mirth at last under control, strode pompously around the laboratory. "This, you will note, my dear sir, is the sole creation of my ancestor. My genius grandfather. Who was vilified and ostracized for the great work he conceived and began in this very room." He halted at the foot of the table and pointed at Kent. "*You* believe Zergopha is a monster. *You* believe Zergopha should never have been brought to life. *You* believe my grandfather was mad. *You* believe *I* am mad!" He laughed again. "*You*, sir, are a damned fool!"

Kent waited for the banjo.

Thor barked instead.

Howe moved up the side of the table, shaking his head with silent merriment, his lips moving soundlessly as if words had finally failed him. When he reached Kent's waist he picked up the hollow egg, held it up to the light, and turned it slowly over in his palm several times.

"Alas, a failure." He grinned and tapped his temple with a finger. "But not a total failure, sir, not a total failure. I have learned from my mistakes, I have gained insight from my persecutors, I have"—and his voice lowered—"the only way to handle the beast in case it should reach us before I have achieved my destiny."

Kent, wide-eyed, listened.

Della, wide-eyed, listened.

Joe Bill woke up and listened.

"Oh yes, Mr. Montana," Howe whispered loudly. "Oh my yes, don't look so surprised. I do know the creature is afoot. But only I know what it is thinking, what are its dreams." He thumped his chest with a fist. "I am the only person on this earth who understands it."

Thor whined.

"But we will not die when it arrives, will we?"

Kent, whose emotions had burrowed somewhere near the attic of his stomach, was confused. If he was going to die, okay, he could live with that; if he wasn't going to die, then why?

"I see you do not understand," Howe said perceptively.

"You aren't blind, I'll give you that," Kent replied with hale Scots bravado, which only earned him another brisk belt on the chest.

"And I do see," Howe said with a manic chuckle. He crushed the egg between his hands and scattered the pieces on the floor. Then he scurried as well as a very tall man with a slight limp could to the refrigerator and pulled out a large jar filled with a crimson liquid. "Do you know what this is?"

Kent shrugged, a clever Highland maneuver which also enabled him to somewhat loosen the bonds from his left hand, the one facing the dog, who immediately trotted over and stared at it.

"It is the secret of our salvation. It is the secret of my fortune. It is the means by which I shall stop Zergopha in its little webbed tracks and then—by God!—I shall *rule the universe*!"

"Poison?" Kent guessed.

Howe laughed.

"A blinding agent?"

Howe fell against the refrigerator in hysterical humor.

"Acid?"

Howe sobered instantly and ran to the table. "No, you damn fool. Do you think I want to destroy the beast? The metaphorical fruit of my loins? The angelic guide of my destiny? Destroy it? End its existence? Are you mad, sir? Have you totally lost your mind?"

I'm missing something here, Kent thought as the mastiff licked his wrist with a sandpaper tongue.

Absently, Howe shoved the animal aside and peered into Kent's eyes. "This jar contains none other than the Fluid of Life, Baron. Can you remember that?"

"Can you say idiot?"

Howe smacked him.

Joe Bill winced.

Howe leaned closer still, his mint julep breath warm on Kent's cheek. "This elixir requires only one remaining ingredient in order to be complete." A forefinger was held up. "One, Baron, and I'll be disappointed in you, sir, if you cannot predict what that is."

Kent sighed. "Me."

Howe laughed evilly, applauded soundlessly. "Almost, almost." He straightened, tugged at his nose, rubbed his cheek. "You, of course, but not all of you."

"Why not take all of me?"

"But Kent," Della cried with an abrupt flash of nurse-training inspiration, "can't you see he's no good without you?" Then she blinked stupidly when she realized she was no longer gagged, blinked stupidly again when Joe Bill put a hushing elbow into her side.

Howe did not notice her partial freedom. "In a way, she's right." A finger stained with many years of experimentation poked Kent just below the sternum. "All I need is one of your organs. A little puree into the Fluid of Life, a little blending of the gene pool in the deep end, and . . ."

Kent waited for it, didn't get it, got it and wished he hadn't, and said, "And you're going to create a mate for the horny bastard outside."

Howe applauded. "Wonderful, Mr. Montana, wonderful!"

Of course, of course, Kent realized, without an accompanying snap of his fingers; Zergopha was a woman, always had been, and the mate—or series of mates considering the female's penchant for snacks between conjugal visits—would contain all the unique aristocratic, physical, and mental superiorities a genuine Scots baron would, quite naturally, have.

The result would be, inevitably, a Super Zergopha.

Hell on wheels and big webbed feet.

Howe applauded again. "You are most certainly no slouch in the deciphering process, Mr. Montana, no sir. I can see that." He touched Kent's chest again. "And all because of your generous donation of a simple vital organ. Which, of course, I am going to get whether you approve of me and my methods or not."

Kent swallowed while, surreptitiously, he further loosened the rope around his right hand, the slobber of the mastiff making it easier than the blood which oozed from where his flesh had been rubbed raw.

"I am, of course, a gentleman, sir," Howe declared with one hand over his heart. "I am a Howe. Therefore, if you survive, I shall let you live."

"And if I don't?"

Howe seemed confused, then chuckled and waggled a finger a him. "Dry Scots wit, sir?"

Kent smiled.

Howe backed away and carefully placed the jar on a shelf behind him. Then he stripped off his jacket, rolled up his sleeves, and opened the drawer of a roll-top desk Kent hadn't noticed before. From it, the man pulled a worn, leather-covered box which, when opened, displayed a dizzying array of surgical appliances whose points and blades and knobs and serrated edges flared starlike throughout the room. With a flourish he picked up a scalpel, held it close to his eyes, winked at his reflection, and blew a kiss to it.

"Naturally, I cannot continue without my assistant."

At which point a woman pirouetted through the door and curtsied.

"Dear Bambi," Howe said, his cavernous voice infused with paternal love.

"Redundant," Kent muttered.

"Sir, you cut me," she scolded coquettishly, and rapped his head with her fan.

"Your lips to God's ears," he told her glumly.

She rapped him again, harder, and skipped to her father's side, exclaimed over the abundant choice of cutting and slicing and separating and holding tools, then danced to the back of the room where, without hesitation, she pulled a heavy tome from its sagging shelf and brought it to the desk, flipped it open, and jabbed a finger at something Kent couldn't see from his current supine position.

"That one," she said to her father. "Let's take that one."

"Excellent choice, Peaches." He scrubbed his hands briskly. "Now, why don't you prepare the subject."

"Boy, I love this part," she said excitedly, rushed over to the table and, as Kent closed his eyes in anticipation of either anesthesia from the fan or a bullet in the brain, ripped open his shirt. "There! All ready."

"What?" he exclaimed, and lifted his head until his chin dug into his chest and nearly throttled him. "Wait a minute! What the bloody hell do you mean, all ready?"

Bambi rather disconcertingly leaned over him and wiggled his chin with thumb and forefinger. "Baron, you mustn't get excited. I'm only doing my job."

He stared at her, stared at her father, looked frantically over to Della and Joe Bill, who were too busy wriggling around in some obscene parody of an impossible love act to notice his plea for help.

His head dropped back heavily.

He heard the Howes whispering by the desk.

And then he heard, much closer than he would have liked had he been given a say in the way things were going, the triumphant cry of some monstrous swamp creature.

"My heavens, Daddy," Bambi said. "My heavens, it's already here!"

The very instant the Howe Clinic ambulance, after sideswiping several parked automobiles and the guard swan, braked to a tire-smoking halt at the foot of the mansion's steps, Roger Ace flung open the rear doors and leapt to the ground, a double-tipped spear brandished lethally in hand. With a cry of "Follow me!" he raced up to the veranda and into the center hall, where Henry Fleuret, having heard the sirens and the crashes, had raced in from the kitchen, fully prepared to oust those who dared crash the party.

"Roger!" the butler/janitor yelled when he recognized the red-faced author with the two doubled-tipped spears.

"Henry!"

"What!?"

"Zergopha!"

A woman screamed and fainted in the front room.

The small army charged in after their leader, weapons at the ready.

"Jonelle! Louisa! Jacques!"

"Father!"

"Uncle!"

"Father!"

Another woman screamed in the front room before Bessy Lou, Doc, and Timmy could be effusively greeted as well, and Henry, confused by all the attention and yelling, slid the doors, shut and demanded to know what in the name of my blue heaven was going on here, did Jacques want his mother to think he had no manners?

Doc told him.

As big as Henry was, he gulped and felt faint, said a silent prayer for his deceased brother, then drew himself together and said, "We must find the sheriff."

"But Mr. Howe—" Roger began.

"—has left on a mission," Henry told him. "But Wally will know what to do."

"If he remembers," Doc muttered bitterly. "That boy's got less brains than Bambi."

Timmy protested loudly at the slur upon his childhood hero, who had saved Thumper and Flower and practically everybody from the terrible forest fire except for his poor momma, and who was pretty darn smart for a deer if he did say so himself.

Bessy Lou clapped him one.

Timmy wailed and hushed.

Then the front room doors slammed open not two seconds before Sheriff Wally Torn passed between them, Blanche Knox hard, and tottering, on his heels and hers.

"There had better be a damn good explanation for this," the lawman warned.

"Zergopha," Doc explained.

With a quick little wave, Blanche tiptoed back into the front room and closed the doors behind her, but not before a woman screamed and fainted.

"Who?" the bewildered sheriff said.

"Aw, c'mon, Wally," Roger pleaded. "The monster, you dope. You know."

Wally scratched his abundant blond hair, his thick neck, his powerful biceps, and finally said, "Oh," as he nodded in dim recognition. "So what about it?"

"He's here!" Doc exclaimed.

Wally spun around, somehow conjuring a .38 Police Special into his hand. "Damn, he's fast!"

"Not here here," said Roger. "Here. In the bayou."

Wally's eyes widened. "Here? In the bayou? Howe's Bayou?"

"Pretty good, thanks," Roger replied, "but that's not the question. The question is—now that the monster's here, and is real, and is threatening the lives of everyone who stays within ten miles of this place—what are we going to do?"

A number of automobile engines started in the driveway.

Several hundred footsteps thundered down the blacktop.

"There is only one thing we can do, now," Wally said in a voice that made everyone stare. And gasp, as he clawed around the base of his neck with his free hand. Jonelle shrieked when she saw a long strip of skin pull loose; Louisa swore in Cajun bewilderment as the sheriff pulled that flap up, higher and higher, until it reached his sturdy jawline; Bessy Lou hid Timmy's eyes with her hand and mumbled a prayer; and Roger nearly dropped his spear when the man suddenly ripped off his entire face and flung it to one side.

"A mask," the doctor said, kneeling down to examine it. "I'll be damned, it's a mask."

"Of course, it's a mask," said the sheriff as he brushed his hair back and rubbed at the bits and pieces of sheriff-colored latex and stringy glue still clinging to his cheeks and brow. "If I hadn't worn a disguise, you would have known immediately who I was."

"Who are you?" Roger asked.

"Wally Torn," the man announced.

"I know that, you look just like him."

Torn raised a cautionary finger. "Not *just* like him, my fast-typing friend. Enough subtle differences so that I could, when I had to, pass unnoticed."

"Hell, you look like Wally to me."

"I am Wally. But not the Wally you think I am. I am"—and he bowed to the ladies, nodded to the men, and winked at little Timmy—"Wally Torn, Special Undercover Agent of the Federal Bureau of Investigation, Science and Climate Control Division." He flashed a badge pinned to the underside of his lapel. "But there is no time for detailed explanations. Suffice to say, I've been watching Howe for a long time, and I guess it's time to call in his chits."

Though all in the hall were stunned at this unexpected revelation that the idiot who had been enforcing their local laws for several years had actually been enforcing Federal law all this time as well, they hastily recovered their composure and set about devising a plan of protection for the mansion while, at the same time, preparing a scheme to trap and take into custody Montague Howe.

As they argued and counter-argued, gesticulated and stamped their feet, Roger glanced down the hall and saw Blanche Knox, shoes daintily in hand, sneak into the library. A second later he heard a muffled shriek, and the clinic receptionist streaked shoeless out of the library and vanished into the ballroom. He frowned, asked Wally to hold up for a minute, and trotted down to the library door. He opened it cautiously. He stepped in warily. He checked to see how many of his latest books Howe kept on the shelves. When he found none—which told him quite a lot he didn't like about the man's character, being as Roger was a writer who could tell a lot about people by the books they read—he searched the rest of the room.

Where, at last, he found the mayor on the club chair. And on the rug. And under a table. And draped over a couch.

He closed his eyes and waited for his gorge to settle before hurrying back to the others.

"The mayor's dead."

"Where?" Wally demanded authoritatively.

"Here and there," the writer told him.

"Damn." The FBI agent shook his head in deep self-recrimination. "My fault, I guess, all my fault. Only this afternoon I gave him the wherewithal to blackmail Howe, after which I was going to arrest him for blackmail and have him run out of office. Backfired pretty badly, I would say."

The front room doors opened wide enough for Blanche to poke a very pale, though not unbecoming considering the makeup she'd chosen, face through.

"Wally?"

"In a while, sugar."

"I'm scared."

He turned and smiled, winked, pointed. "Not to worry, honey lamb. You just wait on me a little longer, I'll explain everything."

She blew him a kiss and vanished.

Roger raised an eyebrow. "Blackmail?"

Torn chuckled. "Informant. She thinks I'm just a big dumb ox. Tells me anything I want to know."

Louisa sighed, and Jacques clapped her one.

Roger, seeing that the agent was more shaken by the mayor's death than he would admit in front of a bunch of people who still thought he looked like Wally Torn, butted one of his spears against the floor and announced that there was no time left to figure out what else was going on around here. Zergopha was on the move; they had to be too.

Accordingly, and to Bessy Lou's misty-eyed adoration, he dispatched Henry Fleuret to round up those guests who hadn't yet bolted, herd them into the ballroom, lock the doors, provide food and drink for their comfort, and tell Herman Quillborn to keep playing until his fingers fell off, then whistle if he had to;

Jonelle and Louisa were dispatched to the kitchen to tell Matilda Fleuret to start boiling water and washing pots in case there were medical emergencies which required a lot of sterile stuff;

Bessy Lou and Timmy were dispatched to the ballroom to keep out of harm's way;

While Roger, Wally, and Doc retired to the rear veranda to set up a routine to patrol the grounds.

But no sooner had they stepped outside and decided to keep the Chinese lanterns burning, when they heard, not too far away, the battle-cry of Zergopha.

"We may be in for it," said Wally as he checked his gun.

Roger sighted along his spears. "The legend says there's only one man who can kill it."

Doc lit a cigarette, took a long pull from his hip flask, and squinted into the shadows scattered across the grass. "Well, if it ain't one of us, we're in deep shit, son."

They fell silent.

They heard the banjo.

They heard a woman try to scream before she was slugged, probably, thought Roger, by Bessy Lou.

Then Henry joined them, a rifle in hand. "We're all set, Wally. Matilda brought in dinner, says no sense in letting it go to waste."

"Good."

"Not really. I can't find Arlaine. I looked all over the house and it looks like she's vanished."

Wally exchanged knowing glances with Roger. "Could be she's gone to warn her father."

"Too late to stop her now," Doc said as Zergopha roared again.

As it may, Roger thought, be too late for us all.

·5·

Della had no idea how things like this worked. She wasn't exactly a hostage, although she couldn't believe that Howe would just
up and kill her, her being the only reliable medical authority the
Landing had, and damn lucky it was to have her; she wasn't precisely a prisoner, since she had been able to free her mouth and
right arm and could probably knock Bambi halfway to Shrove
Tuesday if she had to; and she wasn't, strictly speaking, free,
since her left arm was still pinned beneath the ropes that bound
her and Joe Bill altogether too snugly together.

And Joe Bill wasn't helping with her decision-making contor-
tions either. Every time she tried something, he shook his head,
mumbled incoherently behind his gag, and rolled his eyes in
such a violent way that she couldn't help thinking, in an abstract
physiological sense, that by the time this episode ended he would
probably have eyes in the back of his head, which was fine for
driving that monster Mercury in traffic, but lousy for the poker
games she ran in the back room on Saturday nights.

Zergopha roared.

Joe Bill trembled.

Della pinched him hard on his left hip and whispered that
he'd better pull himself together because the Howes were getting
awfully nervous over there, and they had to do something damn

soon or that tramp from Tara was going to cut out something vital from the baron's innards.

Joe Bill quivered.

Della pinched him doubly hard on his left side and wondered how the hell a man that size with a brain that small could turn out to be such a damn coward.

"Bambi!" Montague said, a quiet urgency in his voice.

"Yes, Father?"

"We'd better hurry, child, or . . ."

Della watched in horror as Bambi skipped back to the baron, smacked him lightly on both cheeks, felt his forehead, and said, "He's still ready, Poppa."

"Like hell," Kent said.

Bambi rapped him with the fan.

Joe Bill shook.

Della snapped her head back and rapped him once on the skull.

Thor trotted to the door, nudged the latch with his massive muzzle, and trotted outside.

With extreme, almost reverent, care, Howe carried the crimson Fluid of Life to a table against the wall and placed the jar in a restraining hoop of glittering steel positioned over a low Bunsen burner flame. Then he drew on a pair of surgical gloves and, with a pair of stainless steel tongs taken from a hook on the wall, removed a large test tube from the refrigerator. This he placed in a wire holder next to the jar.

"Bambi, darlin', would you like the honors? I have to watch the temperature here."

His daughter applauded.

Joe Bill quaked.

Della was out of things to hit him with, and glad she was of it when suddenly the ropes parted with such force that they coiled immediately to the floor. Spain yanked off his gag, leapt from the table, and glared at her. "Would've been out ten minutes ago, you hadn't kept ruining my concentration."

Della smiled weakly.

Bambi cried a warning to her father.

With a curse loud enough to rattle the windows the log cabin laboratory didn't have, Howe spun from his work with a large knife in one hand.

Joe Bill snatched up a long section of rope and advanced on

the plantation-owner-turned-diabolical-scientist.

"You're fired," Howe snarled.

Della, meanwhile, scrambled from the table and ran to help Kent, who suddenly snapped up his free hand and grabbed Bambi's wrist just as she was about to make her initial incision. Her face darkened with fury; his face paled as Della realized that Bambi, despite her costume and flirtatious ways, was a damnsight stronger than she looked.

Zergopha roared.

Joe Bill snapped the rope like a whip, and Howe sliced off a good foot-and-a-half with his knife.

Using a skill of necessity developed in subduing drunks, fighters, and tab-beaters, Della sprang from a standing position over the table that held Kent and wrapped her right arm around Bambi's neck, the intention to bring the woman to the floor, where a good wrestle would soon put her out of the picture. Bambi, however, caught the flying bartender in midair with an elbow, causing her to land on Kent instead.

Kent groaned.

Della clawed and crawled and scratched her way to her knees just as Bambi took aim with the scalpel.

Kent moaned.

Bambi swung.

Della ducked and put a shoulder into the woman's midsection, thus relieving her lungs of having to breathe for a while; a fist took care of the chin, another glanced off the shoulder, and the first recovered enough to plant a decent one just under the left eye.

Bambi tottered backward.

Della leapt.

Joe Bill whipped the rope around again, and again Montague Howe, chuckling confidently, chopped yet another section to the floor at his feet.

Zergopha pounded the wall.

Della, momentarily taken aback by Bambi's strength, wrestled her against the desk, enough papers and pens and miscellaneous scientific apparatus spilling off to make the footing dangerous. Grimly they spun and twisted and danced along the wall, the scalpel between them, first threatening Della's throat, then Bambi's throat, then Della's eye, then Bambi's nose, then Della's neck, then Bambi's ear, then Della's chest, then nothing at all as they reached an impasse by the door, grunting, sweating, groaning, swearing, glaring at each other, smiling humorlessly, promising death with each intensely exchanged gaze.

It was then that Della knew she could not sustain the pace much longer. Her arms were weakening, Bambi's hoop skirt was taking a fearsome toll on her shins, and the scalpel was moving inexorably closer to the vulnerable underside of her determined chin. Within moments she would be dead; within seconds after that she would be a memory. But try as she might, she could not summon that second wind, that reservoir of righteous power, that pool of moral indignation.

Her knees began to buckle.

Her back began to bend.

Bambi leaned over her, lips drawn back in a snarl, eyes narrowed, a moist trace of spittle gathering at the corners of her mouth.

The scalpel in Bambi's hand touched Della's flesh.

The triumphant sound in Bambi's throat chilled Della's blood.

The fist in Bambi's eye snapped her head back viciously, the scalpel away, and the sound to a whimper that lasted only as long as it took for Bambi herself to collide with the wall made of empty cages.

A strong arm wrapped itself around Della's waist and kept her from falling.

A strong voice asked if she was all right.

A strong oath accompanied another fist that met Bambi's recuperative charge and sent it reeling to the floor.

Kent blew on his knuckles.

"Help," cried Joe Bill Spain.

"What took you so long?" Della asked, leaning weakly against the baron, though she wasn't that weak; an advantage, however, if not taken, is not an advantage, which is what her mother, rest her soul, used to say on Friday nights behind the bar.

"She's a woman," Kent said matter-of-factly, nodding to the slowly recovering figure on the floor.

Della leaned back. "You wouldn't hit her because she's a woman?"

"Hey!" Joe Bill yelled.

"Training."

"Sexist bullshit!"

"Chivalry."

"I could have died."

"I had," said Kent, "many years of courtesy, politeness, and door-opening to overcome. One does not simply throw away one's background on a whim."

"A whim?" Della said.

"Yo!" Joe Bill shouted.

"I'm a whim?"

Bambi moaned and, as best as the hoop would permit, struggled to her knees.

Kent smiled. "You were doing all right, as I recall."

Della looked at her right hand. It was a fist. "I was nearly dead."

"And, seeing that, I acted."

"Right. And how," she said sarcastically, "did you manage to act on that whim?"

He shrugged. "I pretended she was my mother."

"Damn it!" Joe Bill screamed.

Della turned, Kent turned, and as one they advanced on Montague Howe, who had trimmed the chauffeur's rope to a mere thread of its former existence and had, even now, begun work on Spain's buttons.

"It's over," Kent told Howe. "Put down the knife."

Howe shook his head in disappointment. "You are a fool, Montana. Dumb enough to be a Yankee."

Della sighed. She had seen such scenes played out in the bar a hundred times a year: the drunk—or, in this particularly odious instance, the villain—refusing to accept defeat, the good guys having to thrash and otherwise convince said villain, or drunk, that that defeat was better than dying, and said villain, or drunk, sometimes taking for damn ever to make up his mind which way the wind blew. Which is why she kept a baseball bat close to hand, for those close calls at the plate. Besides, she was tired, she was hungry, and she couldn't figure out whether being a baron's whim was really worth all this trouble. Unless, of course, she hadn't really been a whim and he was simply using that famed Scots wit to defuse a tense situation.

Suddenly Della had no patience left for philosophical debate. She strode to the table and picked up the Fluid of Life, hissed when the heated glass jar near burned off her fingers, and held it over her head.

"Drop the knife, or I drop the jar."

Howe froze.

Joe Bill sidled away.

"Very good," Kent approved.

"I manage," she said.

Then the door crashed inward, fell off its hinges, and Zergopha crossed the threshold.

Doc Pruit crushed his last cigarette out beneath his shoe and puffed his cheeks as he looked out across the lawn. Behind him, in the ballroom, he could hear the banjo playing a dance tune, could hear laughter, could hear joy, and could not help wondering how easily they forgot that, in the space of a second, their lives could be forfeit on the great altar of amateur science.

Bessy Lou came to stand beside him.

Doc smiled paternally at her. "Are they enjoying themselves?"

The teacher shrugged resignedly. "As best they can, Doc, knowing they could die at any second."

"Ah." He glanced over his shoulder, just in time to see Henry spin by with his wife.

"They're waltzing Matilda right now," Bessy Lou said with a sad, sad smile.

Doc looked at her and, when she finally met his gaze, he knew there would never be another chance to cleanse his pitiful excuse for a soul. "Bessy Lou," he said, "it was I who disgraced your father all those years ago."

Her disbelief was clear.

He looked out over the yard again and in a voice finally overtaken by age and guilt and trying to be heard over the banjo, told her about that dark day so long ago, when he'd gotten young Leigh too drunk to warn the town. It was, he confessed, because he, good old Doc Pruit, had been involved in the first Zergopha experiments. He had provided the first equipment and knowledge. He had encouraged Howe in his possibly satanic explorations of that which man had never explored before in such detail, or with such tragic results.

Her hand took his arm.

Doc swallowed and continued, telling her of his everlasting shame and his subsequent craven refusal to clear the Leigh name, choosing instead to write it all down in his memoirs which, he imagined, Blanche had found by now and was probably figuring a way to make her fortune from them. That she hadn't reckoned on Wally Torn actually being, in real life, the other Wally Torn, most likely would not dissuade her.

"They will be published," he said gloomily, "and the world will know that your family is innocent."

Bessy Lou gripped his hand.

Deep in the bayou Zergopha bellowed.

Roger Ace stepped out onto the veranda and mopped his face with a handkerchief, peered into the evening, and said, "I think I know something you folks don't."

Bessy Lou turned to him without releasing the doctor. "And I know I know something you don't, Rog."

Roger smiled at her with painful love. "And what do you know that I don't, my darling?"

Bessy Lou looked up at Doc.

Doc nodded. What the hell.

She spoke.

Roger listened.

She finished.

Roger said, "Well, hell, Bessy Lou, everybody knows that."

"What?" Doc said.

"Sure. You tell the whole damn thing every Tuesday night in Della Depew's."

Bessy Lou gaped.

"We even got a pool on what time you'll start, what time you'll finish." He grinned. "You think I make enough royalties from *Pirates of the Death Asteroid* to marry Bessy Lou?" He laughed kindly. "I got you clocked to the second, Doc."

"You didn't tell me," Bessy Lou accused.

"I thought you knew," Roger said.

"How would I know?" she answered indignantly. "Do I look like the type of woman who goes to Della Depew's every Tuesday night to listen to a drunken old man spill his guts to the whole town?"

Roger nodded thoughtfully. "You know, Bessy, that never occurred to me."

She smiled her forgiveness. "I forgive you, Roger, seeing as how we're all probably going to die soon."

Doc frowned, scratched his cheek, watched Henry spin by with Matilda again, and said, "So that's what you know that we didn't know? That you already knew?"

"What?"

Doc, with some difficulty considering the time of day and the lack of libation, repeated himself.

"Oh. No. Of course not."

Zergopha howled, somewhat closer than before.

Roger pointed into the dark beyond the reach of the light. "That's what I know."

"Well, hell, Roger," Bessy Lou said in a rare but spontaneous burst of mild profanity, "we knew that."

"You did?"

"Well, so did you."

"Yeah, but I didn't think anyone else could tell."

"Tell what?" Doc asked.

"That that's Zergopha."

Bessy Lou smiled at Doc as if to say *don't mind him, he's a writer, you know,* and patted Roger's arm. "Roger, dearest, why do you think we're holed up in this mansion?"

Roger's eyes fluttered closed, fluttered open, and he said, "Bessy Lou, Doc, that's . . . Zergopha."

Doc waited. So far this boy wasn't exactly making much sense, but then, he never had. Doc had read several of his books and the best he could figure was that folks out there weren't getting enough good sex.

Another wilderness scream.

"And that," Roger announced, "is Zergopha."

Jacques Fleuret joined them at that moment, his shotgun at his side. "I heard it."

"Yep," Doc said. "So did we. Twice."

"No," said Jacques with typical Cajun inscrutability. "What you heard was not what you thought you heard."

"That's exactly what I've been trying to tell them," Roger told the boy gratefully. He took a deep breath. "Now, listen carefully, all of you. I've been observing and stuff—you know how we writers are and all—and it came to me just as I was coming out here to see why Bessy Lou was cuddling up to you,

Doc, that I knew all along something you didn't, but I didn't know it until just then."

Jacques nodded sagely.

Doc fished in his coat for another cigarette or, failing that, a flask he might have forgotten.

"Zergopha," Roger said.

Bessy Lou waited.

Doc waited.

"There are two of them."

Rudy Humpquin sat on the curb outside Della Depew's and wondered what had happened to Silas. One minute the peabrain Watcher was here, the next he was gone; and they was supposed to be drinking their fool heads off about now.

He sighed.

He looked down the street at Myrtle Mae Beauregard marching up and down the white line, rifle in one hand, bowie knife in the other, her shadow from the dim streetlights just about extending to the intersection where Gert Soush was trying to extricate the feet of her armored walker from the manhole cover holes. Ethel June, on the other hand, sat on the hood of a derelict car testing her bugle every ten minutes, once in a while coming close to a fair piece of jazz.

He had been watching for a couple of hours now, and every time he heard Zergopha vent his atavistic spleen back there in the bayou, he considered getting up, going home, packing his bags, and taking the railroad's handcar into Missouri. Then Gert would get one of her legs free, and he didn't think it gentlemanly of him to leave until the show was over.

A faint hum-and-whistle behind him.

"I know, Mort," he said fatalistically, taking a long swig from the bottle he had slipped from behind Della's bar. "Two of them."

A grunt, a truncated sigh, a long exhalation.

Rudy knew the barber was right. With two of the beasts roaming the wild, there was no hope for Howe's Landing. And since Wally was out at the mansion, no doubt getting himself torn all to hell and gone, it was up to the stationmaster to implement the emergency evacuation plans set in place the last time the Union Army came through and burned the place to the ground.

"A fair responsibility, though, Mort," he said.

Mort chortled.

"All right, all right."

He stood, then, and froze in fear when the north sky abruptly turned bright red. A moment later they all heard the explosion.

- VI -

The Shocking
Revelation

As if conjured from the hell of a drunken wizard's spell, Zergopha stood in the log cabin laboratory doorway, panting, puffing, slowly scanning the room as its nightmarish expression decreed that it hadn't the faintest idea was what going on here, but it didn't like it one bit, and somebody, soon, had better explain.

Thor stood loyally at its side, tongue and fangs exposed just in case someone misunderstood.

Bambi, one hand gingerly rubbing her bruised face, scrambled to her feet and hastened to stand beside her father. "Poppa, are we too late?"

Montague Howe put an arm around her shoulders. "It's all right, Peaches, it is quite all right. Have no fear, child, we have been rescued."

"Thank goodness," she said.

"Goodness," said Howe with a mocking glance at Kent, "had nothing to do with it."

Della couldn't believe her eyes, rubbed them with her knuckles, looked again, and still couldn't believe it. "You!" she exclaimed.

• • •

Joe Bill couldn't believe his eyes, but didn't bother to rub them because he knew it wasn't going to make a damn bit of difference. "You?" he queried.

Kent Montana was thoroughly chagrined.

What with everything he had heard, and had overheard, during the past few hours, he knew now that he should have figured this whole thing out long ago. And had he done so, he would have saved himself a great deal of trouble and a ruined silk shirt and white jacket, which were going to be hell to repair if he ever got out of this alive. On the other hand, he hadn't had a good shocking revelation in quite a while, and, since he hadn't figured it out long ago, this certainly qualified as shocking, if not exactly a revelation.

Not that any of it was going to save his life.

"You," he said flatly, once he'd figured it all out and failed to find a way to forget it.

"Yes," said Arlaine Howe. She smiled broadly. "As you can see, it was me all along." The smile faded by sinister degrees. "And now that you know, all of you, I do believe Poppa has some unfinished business he must attend to."

And with that, she began taking off her clothes.

– VII –

Another Shocking
Revelation

Zergopha roared.

Kent blinked. "Your lips didn't move," he said to Arlaine Howe.

He looked at Della. "Her lips didn't move, did they?"

He looked back at Arlaine. "Damnit, your lips didn't move, don't deny it. So how did you do that?"

Arlaine, however, had turned a deathly shade of pale.

Kent looked at Della, looked at Joe Bill, finally looked at Montague Howe, who had frozen in the act of reclaiming the Fluid of Life from Della's grasp.

Oh boy, he thought.

- VIII -

The Chase

· 1 ·

Well, goddamn, Kent thought in disgust; you work your whole life building a body of work for future generations to enjoy, dodging the bullets your mother sends blithely in your direction, roaming the world in search of love and security, and it all comes down to a woman taking off her clothes. Except that she's not really a woman, which proof came when the dress slipped to her feet and he could see that her supply of makeup ran out somewhere around the middle of her bosom. Above said anatomical location there appeared to be perfectly natural, and not entirely undesirable, woman-flesh; below, by contrast, was perfectly natural Zergopha-flesh, scales, red feathers, and what was probably dripping slime.

Bambi threw her sister a towel, and Arlaine quickly scrubbed off the rest of her disguise. Which wouldn't have been so bad if her facial structure had more closely resembled the stunted physiognomy of her reptilian forebears. Unfortunately, she remained all too human except for the scales and the slime stuff, which made her therefore all the more repugnant.

Della shuddered.

Thor whined, whimpered, and despite his master's infuriated command, scrammed.

Montague, scrubbing his hands dryly, fairly beamed in parental admiration and suggested that Bambi run a quick test on the Fluid of Life in order to ensure that the nurse's grimy hands hadn't contaminated the batch.

"Father, please," Arlaine said in a voice that resembled a prolonged, nasty cough, "I don't have much time. It is already the fifteenth day after the first Wailing Moon of the second half of the century." Her black-ridged nails scraped loudly along her sides in a manner Kent supposed would have driven a male Zergopha up the log walls. "I cannot wait much longer." She looked to the doorway.

"Patience," Howe soothed, though it should be noted that he made no attempt to embrace or otherwise comfort her. "As soon as your sister—"

"Ha!" Della said, unable to contain herself or her derision. "Sister? Sister?"

"In a manner of speaking," Howe responded imperturbably. "Remember the gene pool?"

Kent frowned in concentration, looked from one sister to the other, and almost instantly saw the remarkable similarities, although they were certainly much more evident when Arlaine was human.

"Proof," Montague continued, "of my success."

"Ah," said Kent, "but only with a female of the species."

"Exactly. Males have always escaped me."

"Good thing," muttered Joe Bill.

"Then who, or what, is out there?" Kent wanted to know with a demanding point at the nearest wall. Not only to stall for time while he attempted to formulate some clever plan of escape, but also to find out how many more of these damn things there were wandering around here.

"I don't know," Howe admitted.

Della said, "Timmy."

Kent said, "Ah. Timmy."

"Swamp fever," said Joe Bill.

"Timmy?" Bambi said.

"A bright young lad who sought a treasure for his mother, so I am told, and found instead a rather interesting nest. Alas, the egg within that nest had already been hatched."

"Be damned," Howe said to Bambi. "Did you hear that?"

"I thought it was Arlaine," Bambi admitted.

Arlaine swayed, her lidded, hooded, slanted, gold-flecked eyes momentarily glazing over. "Father," she pleaded. And swallowed. And scratched. "Father, please, the call is upon me. I can't—"

"In a minute, Arlaine," Montague snapped. "A Howe is never impatient at the moment of consecration." He turned to Bambi, who was working as rapidly as she could with the Fluid of Life. "Well? Well?"

"Looks all right to me," she decided.

Suddenly Arlaine groaned and reeled. "No time." She panted heavily. "No . . . time."

Montague wrung his hands, looked to the ceiling. "Oh dear." A sharp sigh. A sharper nod. "Well, darlin', if you must, you must, and who am I to deny you? You may have your pick of what's on hand. And who knows? Perhaps we won't need the Fluid after all."

Kent needed neither omen nor playbill to tell him what was next. Arlaine, the human side of her still in control, albeit tenuously, would not race out into the swamp to have at it with a thing that looked like her. No. Of course not. The unholy result of her unholy creation had no doubt given her more than a little taste of civilization and contemporary taste, so to speak. Why, then, have a monster when she could have a baron? Why tumble with a smelly unsightly beast she hadn't even met when she could have a quick roll in the logs with a baron, a post-coital cannibalistic feast of celebration instead of a cigarette . . . and his mother, damn her prickly Highland heart, would win without raising a single imperious finger.

Arlaine moaned.

Della grabbed Kent's arm. "She's in heat."

He nodded.

Arlaine stumbled forward, her hideous arms wide as they sought an embrace with her aristocratic mate.

"She wants to have your child."

He nodded.

Arlaine swatted aside the first table, spilling glass and wood stuff to the floor.

"Pretty badly, I'd say," Della allowed as the second table went the way of the first.

He nodded, and suddenly sprinted to his left, feinted to his right, sprinted to his left again and grabbed the knife Howe had put down in order to check the Fluid of Life. In the same motion, he snapped an arm around the man's neck and placed the edge of the blade just below his quivering chin.

"One step and he dies," Kent warned.

Arlaine hesitated.

"He's bluffing," Howe insisted in a strangled voice. "He can't kill me, Arlaine. He can't kill anyone. He's a baron, damnit, he gets other people to do it for him!"

Bambi, scalpel still in hand, desperately sought a way to slice Kent loose without decapitating her father; Joe Bill hurried to Kent's side with what was left of his rope; Della, seeing that Arlaine might not be fussy about her mating habits this close to the appointed time, hurried to stand by Joe Bill while, at the same time, grabbing the heaviest book she could from a shelf behind her.

"Kill him!" Howe demanded almost hysterically.

Bambi shook her head tearfully.

Arlaine slapped aside the third table in frustration.

"Joe Bill," Kent said urgently, "take Della out of here and get back to the mansion. Warn them. Get some help."

"I can't," the chauffeur said. "Wouldn't be right."

"Damnit, man, do as I say," Kent ordered as Arlaine grabbed a stool and bent the metal post as easily as if she were snapping someone's neck. "I don't know how much longer I can hold her off."

Joe Bill refused. "Can't do that, Baron."

"In God's name, why not?"

"She didn't pick me, I'm gonna slap her around a little."

"Jesus, Joe Bill," Della said, "you're ugly, for Christ's sake. Would you pick you if you were her. It. Whatever?"

Joe Bill shook his head. "Don't matter. The baron's my friend now. I may be ugly, but I don't desert my friends."

"There's a fresh bottle of Glenbannock under my bed," Kent said in desperation.

With a sigh of rather untactful relief, Joe Bill allowed as how his admiration for the baron knew no bounds, that every child between here and Baton Rouge would know of his sacrifice, that every year at this time he would drink a toast to the man's dedication and heroism, that if Della didn't let go, he would leave by himself.

Della kissed Kent's cheek in farewell.

Bambi backed off as Joe Bill threatened her with his thread.

Arlaine snarled when Kent tightened his grip and Howe gasped, his face reddening.

At the door Della looked back, blew a kiss, and vanished into the night.

Joe Bill vowed to return if he could, and vanished into the night.

And Montague Howe, as soon as the others had left, jabbed an elbow into Kent's ribs, thereby bringing down the arm with the knife just long enough for Bambi to lunge forward and cut it with the scalpel.

The knife skidded across the floor.

Kent took a second elbow that allowed Howe to leap to safety beside his daughter.

Arlaine knocked aside the fourth table and lurched forward in an evil parody of sexual abandon and sublime seduction.

Zergopha roared; it sounded farther away.

Arlaine's attention snapped toward the door.

"No!" Howe cried. "No, no, this one, this one!"

Blindly Kent grabbed a jar from the table behind him and threw it at Arlaine. The glass broke against her stomach, and the vile contents, whatever they were, ran down her legs and produced a vile green steam from between her scales.

Arlaine screamed.

Howe leapt on Kent, fists flailing, feet kicking, teeth snapping.

Zergopha called, and Arlaine stumbled lustfully toward the exit.

Kent chopped Howe across the side of the neck.

Bambi ran for the door and grabbed her sister's arm. "No," she begged. "No, Arlaine, please, think of the neighbors."

But Arlaine was lost in rampant lust. She flicked her arm disdainfully and Bambi was flung across the room, hoop spinning, hair uncurling, until she slammed into the wall. Shelves collapsed. Liquids and really nauseating pulpy solids spread across the floor. Sparks jumped. Smoke in thin trails twisted into the air.

She wailed as a beaker with pale green bubbling ingredients spilled on her face.

Distracted, Howe chanced a look.

Emboldened, Kent placed a toe squarely between the man's tailored inseams, and stumbled backward as Howe fell retching and sobbing to his knees.

Zergopha, unless it was Arlaine, yodeled in triumph.

Bambi, still wailing, covered her smoking ravaged face with one hand and staggered to her feet while the other lashed about wildly, knocking jars and vials and test tubes and books and Bunsen burners and papers and trays and surgical instruments onto the floor.

The fire began.

Smoke billowed and thickened.

Charitable instinct and a lack of forethought made Kent reach for Howe's coat to pull him to safety, but the grief-maddened scientist stumbled through the fast-feeding flames to embrace his ill-fated daughter.

Something exploded.

Bambi screamed.

Something else exploded.

Kent reached for and missed the jar that contained the Fluid of Life, which was now boiling so fiercely that its very heat threatened to take the skin from his palm. Yet he understood all too well that leaving it here to the mercy of the unfurling conflagration, would take away the only possible weapon he had. A quick scan of the benches, the tables, the shelves, amid the gathering and deadly acidic fumes, provided him with none too soon with a provident length of blood-spattered canvas he expertly rolled double and flung over the jar. Then, with the prize snuggled safely under his arm, he tripped and staggered and leapt through the flames and smoke and over the tables and the mess on the floor until he reached the door.

A look back then as he gripped the jamb, and he saw the Howes, father and daughter, standing in a proud embrace amid their funeral pyre, their faces nearly destroyed by chemical erosion but their eyes defiant as the fire swiftly expanded about them, and soon obscured them.

"Idiots," Kent muttered and ran into the night.

The log cabin blew up.

• • •

Roger Ace stood on the veranda, spears in hand, and did his best not to scream too loudly when a monster smashed through the stone wall in back and stalked toward the house.

Doc Pruit fell to his knees.

Bessy Lou ran back into the ballroom, crying for Timmy.

Jacques, wondering what Louisa's secret was, brought the shotgun to his shoulder and aimed for the glowing spot between the creature's eyes.

Wally Torn ran out of the ballroom, saw Zergopha standing beneath the Chinese lanterns, and quickly drew his revolver. When Blanche ran out to see what was going on and saw Wally facing the monster, she kissed him long and hard, whispered something into his ear, and ran back inside.

Henry and Matilda spun by.

"Jesus," said Roger, "that thing's damn ugly," drew back his arm, and threw his first spear.

Wally agreed, and fired.

Jacques remembered his uncle Pier and, with tears in his eyes, pulled the trigger.

The banjo stopped.

The acrid stench of gunpowder filled the air.

Several lanterns popped and fizzed and showered sparks to the scorched grass.

An umbrella toppled over.

Zergopha fell against a table but did not fall to the ground.

Wally reloaded.

Roger picked up his second spear.

Jacques reloaded.

Doc Pruit crawled into the ballroom.

Zergopha righted himself and thumped his chest with one fist, shook his spinal feathers in an unmistakable claim to victory, and took another step toward the mansion. Sparks fell about its shoulders. Smoke curled from the soles of its feet.

A woman inside screamed and fainted.

Wally, Jacques, and Roger knew this was their last chance. To fail now would mean their deaths, and the deaths of all those they loved, and a few people they didn't much care about but who didn't deserve to die this way, probably.

"Boys," the pseudo-sheriff said as he took aim again, "I guess this is it."

"You know," Roger said, balancing the spear as he gauged the distance and wind speed, "I once wrote something like this in *The Short War of Mars Station Gazelle*."

"I know," said the young Cajun, who still didn't know what his cousin had been talking about.

"You do?"

"I read it."

"You did?"

"Me too," Wally said.

Roger smiled. Fans. In Howe's Landing, even if one of them was a Fed. If it weren't for the death part, he could die happy about now.

Zergopha charged.

Wally and Jacques fired, and Roger threw his spear.

Zergopha stopped, fell backward, knocked over a table and a chair, rolled onto its stomach, pushed itself to its knees, staggered to its feet, and turned around.

"Well," said Roger.

"Shit," said Wally when the other Zergopha leapt over the wall.

·2·

Once again the intimidating dark made Kent wish he had brought a flashlight. The fire from the explosion had lasted only a few minutes before everything on the tiny island had burned down so low he was no longer able to use its timid light as a guide. He could only hope that he'd be able to keep his feet on the path; otherwise, he'd either trip into the swamp and drown, fall off one of the footbridges and drown, or run into something climbing out of the water and be eaten to death, in which case drowning wasn't all that bad an alternative.

He heard nothing of the Zergophas.

He saw nothing of Della Depew and Joe Bill Spain, which somewhat disappointed him, since he'd been hoping they might think twice about running away before they came back to rescue him. But after the explosion, and the fireball that filled the night sky, and the shock wave that carried him quite easily over the first bridge, he supposed that they supposed he had been killed. He wondered what they would say about him. He wondered how they were going to explain all this to the police.

A match flared not ten feet away.

He threw himself to the ground and tried to cover himself with reeds that were being particularly stubborn about being pulled out by the roots.

"Kent?"

A woman's voice.

Della.

"Kent, is that you?"

"No," he answered as he stood. "It's Zergopha."

The sound of a well-connected slap. "Damnit, Joe Bill, I *told* you it was a stupid idea. Now I'm going to be assaulted by some goddamn critter I don't even know has a first name."

"Well, Arlaine knows me, and I'm still not looking to have a real good time."

Kent brushed himself off and joined them, so pleased at seeing them that he threw his arms around Della and kissed her before announcing himself, an error of judgment paid for by a clout across the head.

"Damn," he said.

"Baron!" Joe Bill said.

Della yanked his face back down and kissed him again, a situation not as unlikely as it sounds, thought Kent, when one considers the lip of the cliff of death upon which they tottered and so grasped for whatever solace they could find.

A volley of gunfire echoed through the bayou.

"All right," he said, "let's go."

"Go?" Della said.

"They need us," he told her sternly. "You for your medical acumen, and Joe Bill for his amazing strength."

A Zergopha roared.

"But you don't owe them nothing," Joe Bill protested as Kent hurried on. "They tricked you into coming out here, they was going to feed you to a woman what ain't no lady, and then they was going to turn you into swamp mulch for the weeds."

"Nevertheless," Kent replied nobly.

He would tell them later that the Howes were dead.

Besides, right now he had to get to the mansion to make sure that neither of the creatures survived long enough to produce other little creatures that would, given the reclusive nature of the swamp and Louisiana politics, thrive and multiply until it was too late for anyone to stop them. The burden he had tucked beneath his arm would, he prayed, be just the thing.

If it wasn't, there was always Spain's faithful Mercury and the fastest road out of the parish.

Joe Bill struck another match and took them over a bridge.

Della whispered a question about the fate of the Howes.

Kent whispered back only that the Howes were doing just fine where they were.

Della wanted to know what he had under his arm.

"Sweat," Kent told her, "and damn tacky of you to mention it."

She jabbed a finger at the canvas. "That, dope. What is it?"

They made it across the next two bridges without incident, although Joe Bill did burn his fingers and accordingly dropped all the matches into the swamp.

Zergopha's battle cry echoed through the trees.

Night creatures cried back.

Invisible things flitted through the dark.

At the last bridge they were rewarded with bright flickering light from the Manor's backyard.

"In time, I hope," Kent told them, and hurried across, not at all as confident as he hoped he sounded, which wasn't very, given the expression on Joe Bill's face as he joined him on the other side.

Della was halfway over when the bridge collapsed.

"Momma," Timmy said from the ballroom, "what are they doing?"

"They're defending us," Bessy Lou told him in a choked voice.

"No, not them, the gophers."

Bessy Lou looked, saw what the Zergophas were doing in the middle of the yard, and clapped her son a good one.

Wally reloaded his last bullet.

Jacques held his rifle like a baseball bat.

Roger figured he could lift one of the white chairs if it wasn't too heavy.

Doc Pruit returned abashed at his cowardly retreat, looked off the veranda, and said, "Lord, you really think they were meant to do it that way?"

Without thinking twice, Kent shoved the Fluid of Life bundle into Spain's astonished arms and plunged into the swamp. Though the water itself wasn't more than neck deep in the middle of the channel, the primordial mud below had such qualities of tenacious suction that Della was barely able to move, and the more she struggled, the lower she sank. Kent had also spotted agitated swirls and splashes a few dozen yards to his left that told him the nurse hadn't long to stay in one piece.

He swam, then, in a self-developed doggie-paddle that soon brought him panting to her side. "Get on," he said, and spit water.

"You're kidding."

He jerked his head toward something floating lazily toward them out of the shadows. "Get on!"

She got on.

He hadn't exactly meant her to straddle him, but as long as he was able to keep his head above water he supposed it didn't matter as long as they reached the other side without undue predator interference. Not terribly elegant, however. A little on the ludicrous side, actually. But his hands and feet, spurred by the alligator drawn to the commotion, worked wonders to behold, and did double duty when yet another creature slipped off a bank to his right.

Della gripped his hair and urged him on.

Joe Bill ran to the water's edge but ran no farther when he spotted the reptiles.

Kent, his eyes on the chauffeur and the solid comfort of the bank, swam for his life, spitting brackish water, feeling himself grow bald where Della held him, feeling his arms tire and his legs begin to sheath themselves in lead.

The alligators submerged.

Della thumped his back.

Joe Bill cried a warning.

Kent suddenly took a deep breath, dove, tucked, bucked, felt the weight on his spine vanish, and surfaced just in time to see the plucky drenched nurse sprawl safely onto the bank. Then he struck out again and had just reached out for Joe Bill's hand when Della screamed.

He looked.

An alligator looked back.

Kent kicked it on the snout.

Incensed and stung, the alligator whipped sideways into its companion, which immediately figured a bird in the claw and buried its teeth into the first gator's exposed belly.

Kent climbed ashore and knelt there, gasping and coughing.
A gunshot from beyond the wall.

It never ends, he thought; it never ends.

The chauffeur helped him to his feet; Della, weeping with joy,
supported him with an arm around his waist; and the three of
them passed through the gate just as Arlaine jumped Zergopha's
bones.

Joe Bill screamed in horror.

Della could only stare.

Kent, after telling himself that there was no place like home
and this sure wasn't it, darted through the garden, stripping the
canvas from the jar as he went. Someone yelled at him from
the veranda, but he could neither see nor understand, and it
didn't matter anyway because the two man-made monsters rolling about on the lawn had discovered his presence.

There was no time for a test.

He moved as close as he dared without becoming an unwilling
trois in the animalistic *ménage* and, with a prayer, threw the
Fluid of Life over them both.

The yard fell silent.

Kent stumbled back a few paces.

And then, without warning, the creatures vented a high-
pitched, heart-rending scream.

They lunged apart.

They lunged together.

Their scales rippled and folded and curled up and fell off;
their feathers straightened and quivered and stiffened and fell
off; the webbing between their fingers and toes thickened and
fell off; their teeth fell out.

They attempted to stand, and could not, and fell back into each
other's scrawny, powerless arms.

Della came up to stand beside him. "That's really disgusting,"
she said. "What was it?"

"Howe's formula," he told her, and turned away, unable to
bear the sight any longer. He put an arm around her waist and
began walking toward the manor. "It was a gamble."

"You mean you dumped the Fluid of Life on them?"

He nodded. "I had to. I had no acid, which I had seen, as
you know, burn Arlaine, and from the sound of things, ordinary
firearms had no effect." He shrugged. "I had no choice."

They looked back.

Arlaine and her Zergopha were little more than bones bleached by the light of the exploding Chinese lanterns.

"Howe couldn't wait decades for them to mature and mate, as his grandfather had. Waited, that is," Kent explained as the others wandered out from the mansion and gathered around mutely, shocked, disheveled, numb with relief. "I ascertained that the Fluid of Life was actually an agent to speed things up, hurry things along, manipulate the growth process. If Howe had had his way, we would all be dead, and he would have had an army of a thousand Zergophas before the year was out." He wiped his face with the back of his hand. "I reckoned that the Fluid of Life would become the Fluid of Death if it could somehow get inside them." His smile was almost rueful. "The way they were . . . sort of . . ."

"Wow," Timmy whispered in awe.

"Oh," said Roger. "You mean lovebites and lustscratches, things like that."

Bessy Lou clapped him.

Kent nodded anyway. "All it took was a good dose. You can see the results."

The last lantern exploded, and there was nothing left but the golden light spilling from the ballroom, and the light of the Louisiana moon.

The banjo played a single note.

"That," said Della Depew, "is the dumbest thing I've ever heard in my life."

·3·

They sat on the front porch steps, mint juleps well in hand, while the victory celebration continued around them. A jubilant telephone call from Henry brought Rudy Humpquin and the militia in from town, the banjo had found a soulmate in Ethel June's bugle, Gert was a sensation with the silver taps Joe Bill had put on her walker, and from the sound of it now, no one was going to quit until Christmas.

The door opened. Wally Torn and Blanche Knox came out arm-in-arm, walked down to the driveway, and stopped.

"You did good," the sheriff said. "I'm grateful."

Kent waved him an embarrassed *go on you're just saying that*.

" 'Course, you realize I can't report none of this. I don't truly believe anyone would believe it."

"Don't worry about it," Kent said. "But what are you going to do now? The mayor's dead, the Howes are dead, it looks like your job is finished here."

Wally winked. "Not to worry about this ol' country boy, Baron." He pinched his own cheeks, then pinched one of Blanche's. "Sweet dumplin' here, she found my face in a planter, fixed it up. I think I'll just go on being good old Wally Torn, Howe's Landing's duly appointed sheriff. Hell, ain't nobody gonna know the difference."

"Wally," Blanche said impatiently.

"Okay, sugar, okay." He shook Kent's hand. "You take it slow, you hear?"

Kent smiled.

Blanche told her lover to stop jawing like a hick and put his face on so they could go; her lover told her he already had his face on; she told him it didn't look right, maybe they should go back to the clinic for an examination; he told her he was still on duty, he couldn't take his guns off.

"Oh my," Blanche said, fanning herself. "Oh my."

Kent looked up then, at the porch ceiling, and frowned as he tried to identify a faint but persistent tapping.

Della laughed quietly. "That's a typewriter you hear."

"Now?"

"That's right. Roger, hot at his new book. Says it'll make him a million and he and Bessy Lou and Timmy can live the rest of their lives in luxury."

"How pleasant for them."

A child's cry, a bird's angry response, and the fading sound of panicked running feet.

"Remind me," Kent said, "to leave my fortune to that swan." They drank.

They listened to the music.

"I imagine the Bayou Blast is no longer."

"I guess so," Della said. "Turns out, according to the new mayor, Thurly Rille, the only backers were old Stonewall and Montague. A scam from the beginning."

"So your land is safe."

"Always was, Baron, always was."

They drank.

They sighed contentedly.

Kent considered returning to New York to strangle his agent, and decided it wouldn't be worth it. He could only hope that something else would come along fairly soon to lift him out of the artistic depression he tripped into once all the excitement had subsided. He hated to think that after all these years, his mother had been right, that he had no business being an actor when the family estate needed looking after.

He leaned back against the porch post, drew his legs up, and glanced inside just in time to see Doc Pruit prance by with Gert Soush sans walker, an uncharacteristic flush of joy on the old man's face.

Swell.

Boy gets girl, boy gets girl, boy gets girl, swan gets boy, boy gets girl cousin who really isn't a cousin but is most definitely a girl, and I get fired from a job I didn't even have in the first place.

Swell.

Della, looking at him from her place against the opposite post, held up her glass. "So now what?"

He lifted a shoulder and winced. "I don't know. I ache, I'm cut, I'm bruised all to hell and gone, I'm out of work, I'm out of Glenbannock because Joe Bill has a memory like an elephant, and I smell like a swamp."

"That *is* the swamp."

"Aye," he said, "and welcome you are to it."

Silence, except for the swan and Timmy making their fourth or fifth circuit of the mansion.

"Well, I can't give you a job," she said at last. "I don't need a bartender. And my liquor isn't anything like that stuff that's got Joe Bill mulching roses in the chandelier." A lopsided smile, then. "But, in case y'all have forgotten, I am a nurse."

He had.

He felt like a jerk.

He felt like leaping up and clicking his heels when he heard, in the distance, a familiar sound.

"What's that?" Della said.

"Salvation," he told her, and blew a kiss at her puzzled expression.

Within moments a spiffy red motor scooter ridden by a man in western boots, jeans, a denim jacket, and a worn but lovable grey western hat, rode up to the foot of the steps and stopped on a dime Timmy had dropped the last time around.

"I never thought you'd get here," Kent said warmly, reaching for the package the man handed to him.

"Montana," the man said as he turned to ride away, "you'd better read about the Bruce and the spider again, or you'll be a nervous wreck by the time we're done."

A wave, a blown kiss to Della, and the messenger disappeared into the night.

Della rested her chin on her knees. "Your next script, huh?"

Kent nodded, opened it, looked at the first page, and emptied his glass in a single gulp.

"Epic?" she asked somewhat wistfully.

"I should live so long, as my agent says. Have you ever heard of Lon Chaney, Bela Lugosi, people like that?"

She frowned, then nodded. "Sure."

The banjo played a chord.

"Vampires and werewolves, things like that, right?"

Kent nodded woefully.

"But not in Louisiana, right again?"

After a brief hesitation, he nodded again.

Rudy Humpquin poked his head out the door. "Train don't leave until Monday, y'know." And was gone.

Della crawled over to him, rested her arms on his knees, and looked him so close in the eye he had to lean away. "Well," she said, "I guess you're going to need a physical before you can play that new part, whatever it is."

He blinked.

She sighed.

He smiled.

She giggled.

He tapped the script and said, "But no biting."

She bit him.

And Joe Bill whistled "Dixie" as he fell from the chandelier.

THE CREDITS

Producer	Northgate 386/20
Director	Lionel Fenn
Writer	Lionel Fenn
Editor	Ginjer Buchanan
Titles	Susan Allison
Transportation	'86 Thunderbird
Gator Wrangler	Burt Tilstrom
Dialect coach	Joe R. Lansdale
Driver	Clint Eastwood
Doctor	John
Nursing services	Tara Tarkington
Creative Financial Inc. services	Bryan Webb
Swan	Lynn
Suits provided by	Party of the first part
Antebellum gowns by	Gila Queen's New Orleans Busty Lust Shoppe
Primordial Swamp provided by	Exxon

AND SPECIAL THANKS TO:

Thomas Jefferson, for buying Louisiana in the first place, and Robert Petitt, for sending the map that shows where it is in the second place; the Kent Montana Fan Club; and the Office of the Mayor, Howe's Landing, Louisiana, without whose help the train wouldn't have stopped on Monday and we'd all still be there, listening to that damn banjo.